WHAT A MATCH

MIMI GRACE

CONTENT NOTE

- This book contains a number of sexually explicit scenes

Chapter One

KISSES ARE SIMPLE. The good ones all start the same. First, a person must look deeply into their potential kissing partner's eyes. Then, spare their mouth a glance to make intentions clear. As distractions fade and imaginary music swells, desire propels them closer. Finally, both muster up the courage to lean in and let their lips connect.

Gwen Gilmore was expecting such a routine tonight. It was why, despite being famished from a long day at work, she'd skipped the onion-laced hot dog at the concession stand for a sensible bag of popcorn. The kernels rattled around her empty stomach, but the cheering crowd and the burly men chasing a puck across the ice were a gracious distraction.

She looked at her date, Cameron. If his jostling knee and occasional elbow to her side was any indication, he was completely absorbed in the game.

During their first date, she'd been pleased to learn he checked off several qualities on her List. He was accomplished (a tech guy), passionate about something (the ethics surrounding artificial intelligence), and could talk at length about a book not written by a misogynist (a blessing).

The sports fan thing had taken her unawares, but she decided it gave him a little… pizzazz.

"Do your fucking job, man!" Cameron shouted, jumping to his feet to point at the referee on the ice as Gwen dodged his flailing scarf.

If everything played out according to her plan, they'd have their first kiss tonight. Then they'd set up their third date, and by the end of the month, she'd invite him to brunch with her parents.

A loud buzzer went off, ending the first half of the game. People left their seats to stretch their limbs and use the washroom. Meanwhile, a mascot arrived on the ice and danced underneath the jumbotron playing sponsored ads.

"That was obviously a foul back there," Cameron said, retaking his seat. "How are you enjoying your very first live hockey game?"

She'd watched several matches on TV over the years. It was the national sport; it was inescapable. But she'd never collected stats or paid attention to the names of popular players. However, she'd come prepared with an arsenal of knowledge she'd learned online the night before.

"It's great," Gwen said. "I'm really impressed with their backchecking. Very efficient."

Cameron nodded.

"And that Randy guy is pretty good, right?" Gwen continued. "You saw how he made that penalty shot?"

Her date's expression soured slightly, and it took Gwen a couple of seconds to figure out why.

Wrong team. *Shit.*

"But we're still kicking their asses," she said quickly.

"Hell yeah, we are!" Cameron said, chucking his fist in the air.

They'd have to do something more up her lane for their next date.

When halftime officially ended, Cameron's attention returned to the players, and the game progressed and concluded as most games did, with one team victorious. The arena burst into cheers, and Gwen found herself high-fiving strangers and shouting a chant she was hearing for the first time.

Hundreds of jubilant spectators and Gwen proceeded on a slow shuffle to the exit. Cameron chattered with the people around them while Gwen reapplied her Chapstick and threw back no less than a dozen Tic Tacs.

When they finally left the closed confines of the arena, all the noise and glee faded as patrons scattered across the expansive parking lot.

Gwen and Cameron finally made eye contact, and she stepped closer to him as they strolled toward her car.

"Great night," she said.

She couldn't have asked for better ambiance for a first kiss. Crisp early fall air and a clear sky decorated with stars and a full moon.

When they arrived at her car, she turned to Cameron, ready to say all the things she usually said after dates. But there was no need to because he was already puckering his lips. She smiled as they inched closer to one another.

This was it.

This would solidify everything and move them toward an end goal Gwen wouldn't dare daydream about yet.

When their lips finally met, the noise that should've melted away with the kiss sharpened instead. It was hard to say when Gwen realized she wasn't enjoying herself, but if she were to take a guess, it was somewhere between their teeth clashing and when she felt Cameron's tongue on her chin. Things devolved further when it became clear she would not get a breath for the duration of the kiss.

Thirty something-year-old woman steps out on a cool Friday night to find a mate, gets mauled by a prospect.

When they parted, all Gwen wanted to do was run the sleeve of her coat across her mouth, but she forced her arms to remain flush at her sides.

That had to be the second-worst kiss she'd ever experienced. The absolute worst one was with Trey Freeman, but they had been fifteen years old.

"Do you want to come over?" Cameron asked intently.

Over where? Surely not his place where they'd likely do more than exchange sloppy kisses.

"I've had a long day. I should be getting home," she said.

Cameron nodded, clearly disappointed.

"Tons of papers to mark," she said, committed to some unknown benevolent reason to give his pride the softest place to land.

"I'll text you later then," he said.

She should've told him that wouldn't be necessary, given him the respect of calling things off face-to-face, but her brain couldn't construct a sensitive reply because it was still screaming at her about the chin spit.

After scrubbing off layers of skin with a makeup wipe, Gwen ended up careening into the parking lot of her local 7-Eleven fifteen minutes later. She took her time under the harsh lights of the store to narrow down the type of potato chips to buy.

In the checkout line, she ran over her weekend's to-do list in her head and eyed the taquitos in the heated glass case on the counter. But her attempt to temporarily forget the night's events was sidelined when the couple directly in front of her started acting up.

They held each other and rubbed up on one another like they were trying to start a fire. Fervent whispers were exchanged just before they began making out with game show host-level enthusiasm.

"Yup, let's do that," Gwen said under her breath as she turned to stare at the churning Slurpee machines instead.

Gwen knew buried underneath her annoyance was jealousy. *She* wanted to be obnoxiously affectionate with someone in public.

When she finally arrived home with her dinner and was struggling to unlock her apartment, she felt the eyes of the lady next door. She knew the older woman was standing in her bathrobe, peering out of the peephole.

"Good evening, Brenda," Gwen said into the empty hallway.

The woman didn't even pretend not to be watching because the next thing Gwen heard was the chain door guard disengaging.

Brenda was a busybody through and through and made it her business to be in everyone else's.

"Long day?" the woman asked once she'd stepped into the hallway in her bathrobe.

"The longest."

"Hmm."

God only knew what conclusion or tally she was making in her head.

"Before you go, dear, I have a package with your address." The older woman dipped back into her apartment and reemerged with a sizable box. "They must've gotten our numbers mixed up."

Gwen immediately knew what it was.

"Thanks," she said, retrieving the package from the lady. She knew the law alone was the only reason it wasn't open.

Once locked in her quiet apartment, Gwen removed her boots and outerwear and stared at the package that held her ex-boyfriend's belongings. "Return To Sender" was written on top in black marker.

An omen, perhaps.

She shoved the box into the corner near the front door and mentally made a note to text him for his correct address. It would have to be done in the morning. If she did it now, she knew they'd end up having phone sex, and that always left her feeling weird.

While she ate her food, she split her attention between her favorite local daytime talk show and a half-completed crossword puzzle.

"Could the state of your sock drawer be hurting your relationship?" one of the hosts of the morning show asked. "A Swedish hygge expert says *ja*."

Soon, however, the puzzle and the banter between the hosts lost her interest as the disappointment of yet another failed date crept in.

After cleaning up her dinner, she stood in front of the calendar affixed to the fridge and drew an "X" through that day's box.

She flipped through the pages, seeing similar Xs she'd drawn. For some reason, time had felt unmoving. Like it was patiently waiting for her to get her love life in check before resuming. But the truth was laid out plainly on her tree-themed calendar. She'd been at this dating thing for six months.

Her plan had been to put herself out there as much as possible and only pick guys who met at least three qualities on her List. It was a strategy she'd thought would have her boo'd up by winter.

Well, with months of dating under her belt, she had

nothing to show for it except one incredibly mediocre one-night stand and a dozen coffee shop receipts.

It all left her feeling weary and despondent, and she didn't know how many more dead-end text conversations she had left in her.

Something had to give.

———

"Yes, my sweet little butterflies, feel the movement from within your soul! Never doubt that there is something inside wanting to come out. It can be ugly. It can be weird. Just let it out!"

Gwen looked up from the canvas to witness the art instructor swing her arms to and fro while the big feathers in her hair danced along. She'd yet to give advice or instruction Gwen found even remotely helpful.

"She isn't a real painter, is she?" Gwen asked her mother, who sat beside her.

The older woman had convinced her painting and sipping wine with other people in a chain restaurant was a good use of their time.

"No, no, she is," her mom said, flicking her brush against the canvas. "I went to her exhibit last summer."

"Of course you did."

Her mom, a soon-to-be-retired social studies teacher, had always had an appreciation for the arts. Gwen turned back to her painting and resumed the struggle to get a particular line straight.

"Baby, you know you're not getting credit for this," her mom said, looking over. "It's just for fun."

Gwen pulled back and studied the lighthouse that was coming along. "I am having fun."

"Fun-ish" was more accurate. A mere nine months

ago, she wouldn't have thought that she'd be spending a Saturday afternoon with her mom doing arts and crafts.

The demise of her long-term relationship had coincided with her parents' long-overdue divorce, and it meant she and her mother had been hanging out more.

"Don't look now," her mom whispered suddenly. "But I think the young man across from us is looking at you."

Gwen froze and slowly tilted her head past her canvas to see who her mother was talking about. Her mom's definition of a "young man" was anyone who couldn't name all the members of The Commodores, but this one was at least around her age *and* attractive.

"Ma, he's wearing a wedding ring, and he's not interested in me. He's just watching the TV behind us."

Her mother gave the man another look then located the television playing the highlights from last night's hockey game.

"And it wouldn't matter even if he *were* single and interested," Gwen said.

"Why? You have something against handsome men?"

"No, because I'm taking a dating sabbatical."

Her mother stilled. "A what?"

"A dating sabba—"

"Now, why in the world would you do that?"

"Do you know I caught myself unironically using the term 'Mr. Right'?" Gwen asked. "I'm a cliché. A woman in her thirties obsessed with finding a husband. It's pathetic."

"And spending your Saturday in a Chili's painting a lopsided lighthouse with your mother is?"

Gwen looked at her picture. "What do you mean 'lopsided'?"

"What I'm saying is you can't give up on love because you had a few disappointing outings."

Not disappointing. Disappointing was how Gwen

would describe the salads she'd sometimes eat for lunch or her childhood cat's emotional availability. Sure, she'd had bad dates before, but there was something about the one last night that kind of felt like hitting a wall.

"You know what it is? You're putting too much pressure on these men *and* yourself," her mom said. "People are not going to check off everything on that list of yours. And they don't have to for things to work."

"Maybe. But for now, I'm taking a break," Gwen said.

Stepping back might get her excited and hopeful again. Her mom continued to stare at her.

"What?"

"I'm going to suggest something, and I want you to have an open mind."

"I'm not growing out my hair."

(Another post-breakup change.)

"It's not that," her mom said.

"Okay, then. Consider my mind officially open," Gwen said, meeting her gaze.

"Why don't you hire a professional matchmaker?"

Gwen blinked. "I think maybe for the same reason I haven't tattooed 'lonely woman' on my forehead yet?"

"They'll take your wants and needs into consideration before pairing you up. And you know you've always been very… particular."

"You can say picky."

"No. That sounds negative, and there's nothing wrong with being selective, except it takes time to sort through random men in this big of a city."

Ah, yes. That bitch, Time.

"At this point, just call me an old hag," Gwen said.

Her mom placed her hand on Gwen's knee. "Eric was lightning in a bottle, and maybe doing this will help you recapture it with someone else."

Hearing her ex's name was a jolt to Gwen's system. She and Eric met through mutual friends several years ago and, at one point, had been very compatible. She would like to find that again, but a little more permanent.

Maybe her mother was right.

If she took all the methods of finding a partner into consideration, a matchmaker would be most in line with her personality. There was no guesswork and half-baked adages like "follow your heart" to cling to.

She could hand over a list of things she wanted in a mate, and voilà—her perfect match. The fact that she hadn't even considered it before now was astonishing.

A grin slowly stretched across her mother's face.

"I'm not committing to anything yet, but I'll look into it," Gwen said.

"No need," her mom said as she dove into her purse and emerged with a card.

"What's that?"

"It's the contact information for a reputable match-making agency. Baby, Mr. Right better get ready."

Chapter Two

BEFORE ANTHONY WOODS pulled up to his apartment complex, he thought the worst part of his day had been the stale oatmeal raisin cookie he'd eaten at breakfast. But then he arrived home and found his neighbors in a huddle in front of the building's entrance, and it didn't bode well for the relaxing evening he'd been anticipating.

Approaching the group, he spotted his landlords, brothers with wiry hair and ill-fitting coats, trying to talk to the agitated crowd.

Anthony turned to one of his neighbors filming the scene with his smartphone. The two had never talked, but Anthony had deduced he was a city bus driver from the uniform he usually wore.

"What's going on?" Anthony asked.

"Some bullshit, that's what," the man said, his eyes not leaving the screen. "Recording everything just in case."

One of the landlords geared up to say something when the noise ebbed, but another rush of incoherent questions cut him off.

This was ridiculous.

Anthony whistled sharply, and the people slapped their hands over their ears and fell silent.

"Okay," the taller landlord said. "As I was saying, the heating system is broken, and because of the dipping temperatures, by law, we can't let you stay here until it's—"

"Didn't you do maintenance on it last year?" someone asked.

"That was the plumbing—"

"How long is it gonna take to fix?"

"Well, that depends entirely on—"

"How long?"

"Four weeks," one of the landlords said.

There was rumbling in the crowd.

"Possibly six."

The groaning swelled and protests erupted, and Anthony couldn't help but join in now. His days were consumed with running his boxing gym, and he looked forward to coming home and icing his joints in his quiet apartment.

"Our stuff," Anthony bellowed, cutting through the noise with his strong voice. "Can we get our things?"

This question quietened the crowd once again.

"Yes, you have an hour to collect what you need."

The process from there on out became a lot smoother. Anthony packed his belongings into a suitcase and a duffle bag, cleared out the perishables in his fridge, and unplugged the appliances.

After exiting the building, he opted to stay behind and help the others. He dumped bags into trunks and back-seats. Carried strollers and toboggans to tie on top of mini-vans. And let a mom of two scold him for his lack of appropriate outerwear. By the time he entered his own vehicle, not only was it dark, but he couldn't feel his fingers or toes.

As he blew into his cupped hands and waited for his vehicle to heat up, he thought of his options. It was late enough in the evening that he didn't feel comfortable calling anyone up.

So he searched for the closest and cheapest hotel with no bed bugs or ghosts and tried to end his day on a better note.

While eating takeout in front of the TV in a room the front desk clerk guaranteed had no vermin or supernatural activity, a ping on his phone alerted him to all the different transactions he'd made in the last hour.

He realized then he wouldn't be able to stay here for a month or more. The landlords would probably be required to compensate all apartment residents for the displacement, but Anthony knew there'd be a cap. Being an owner of a small business a little over a year old meant he didn't have the luxury of unplanned spending.

He'd have to ask for help, sleep on someone's couch or something. He was already dreading the task. After a childhood of "be seen, not heard," living alone was preferable, and he'd been doing it since he was seventeen. But what choice did he have?

That night, Anthony tossed and turned and had a nightmare that his entire apartment building grew literal wings and flew off into the ether.

The following morning, he headed into work, hauling his suitcase and duffle bag. His gym, Spotlight Boxing Studio, was his dream realized, and for better or for worse, this place made up a big portion of his identity and worth. He hoped he'd have the privilege of seeing the red and white sign outside grow weather-beaten.

When he entered the building, he found his best friend and business partner in the staff room deep inside the refrigerator.

"How many kinds of yogurt do we need to keep in stock, do you think?" Duncan asked as he emerged from the appliance, holding three different types of yogurt.

"One is soy-based, one is Greek, and one is actually good."

Duncan moved to return the food to the fridge but stopped short when he saw the bags in Anthony's hands. "You leaving me? After all we've been through?"

Anthony rolled his eyes. "The heat is out at my apartment. Won't be fixed for a while."

"Damn. Where you staying?"

This man was his best friend—someone he could trust in business and life. If there was anyone who would be more than willing to help him, it was Duncan. But it still felt uncomfortable.

"Actually, I was wondering if I could crash at your place," Anthony said.

"Of course, brother. I'll have to run it by Retta, but I'm sure it's fine."

"Yeah, and if not, I'll figure out a hotel or something."

"Stop. You're not paying for a hotel. I know how much you make," Duncan said, and Anthony dropped his bags and grabbed what he needed to make his protein shake.

"Speaking of knowing how much you make," Duncan said, nodding to a stack of mail on the counter.

No doubt most of them were bills. The cost of running this place was humbling. They weren't struggling per se, but they weren't thriving either. As a professional boxer, Anthony had been used to training and "mind over matter"-ing his way to victory. But despite how much effort and hours he and Duncan poured into the business, success was anything but guaranteed.

The sound of voices and laughter drifted from the front of the gym, alerting the two men that the other trainers had arrived. Their team was another reason Anthony and Duncan needed to make this thing work.

"Maybe we should cut down on the three-different-yogurt thing," Duncan commented glibly.

"If that's all it took," Anthony said, "I'd throw out the whole damn refrigerator."

———

With the idea of hiring a matchmaker firmly planted in Gwen's head, she got kind of obsessed and started looking up every single matchmaking service in the city.

From her research, she found an agency where participants only met during lunchtime for fifteen minutes. Then there was one where it seemed like retirement savings and blood oaths were membership requirements. And another where the word "elite" was used just enough times to irritate her.

In the end, the company her mother had suggested was the best.

Hearts Collide Matchmaking Service didn't feel like a glorified dating app, but the premium cost meant that her summer vacation to somewhere with a beach wouldn't happen next year.

That is, if she got accepted into the program.

"So? What do you think?" Gwen asked her best friend, Raven, who she'd lured away from her post as the school's receptionist with an autumnal Starbucks drink.

Raven sat on the edge of Gwen's classroom desk, reading the matchmaking application she hadn't yet built up the nerve to submit.

"I thought your favorite color was taupe, not yellow," Raven said, popping her bright pink bubble gum.

"It is, but it makes me sound boring. But never mind that, what do you think about it overall?"

"Thorough. Very thorough," Raven said. "But I'm not a fan of the picture."

"Well, that's my face," Gwen said, walking over to take another look at the selfie she'd attached. It adhered to the requirements detailed on the application.

"It's not your face, it's the angle. Like, I'm not sure if you're looking for love or renewing your passport, babe."

"I don't know what you want me to do about that," Gwen said.

Raven rose from the table. "Stand against the wall. I'm taking a better one for you."

Unwilling to put up a fight this early in the morning, Gwen got in front of the whiteboard.

"Okay, pout," Raven said as she aimed the lens at Gwen.

"Pout?"

"Yes, like——" She pushed out her glossy red lips.

"I'm not doing that," Gwen said, shaking her head.

"Okay, fine. Then prepare for those matchmakers to see the photo you chose and think,

'Did this chick really submit her mug shot?'"

Resigned, Gwen did her best to replicate her friend's expression.

"Great, all right," Raven said. "I want you to make it more subtle this time. Think about sucking through a straw that you're holding lightly between your lips."

She adjusted her mouth accordingly.

"Now squint a little like you're trying to read a menu on the wall, but you haven't gotten your glasses prescription checked in a while."

The instructions were odd and very specific, but the

result was pictures that were better than the dozens Gwen had taken in her living room a day before.

"See? I'm a professional. I know what I'm talking about," Raven said, tossing her big bouncy hair.

Gwen gave her friend a look.

"Shut up," Raven said. "It counts. Three months of hand modeling counts."

After replacing her application photo, Gwen said, "Okay, I'm sending it." She shut her eyes and brought her finger down on the submit button before throwing her phone into her desk drawer like it was a burning piece of coal.

"Now try to relax, okay?" Raven said, coming over to place her hands on Gwen's shoulders. "If you want, I can set up an appointment with my astrologer for a reading."

Gwen shook her head. "No, I'm good. Her accuracy scares me, and I'd rather live in delusion for a little bit."

"There's no delusion. You're going to have fun, find love, and live happily ever after."

Gwen nodded. She needed to hear those positive words regardless of how frivolous they were. Initially, she'd been reluctant about the whole idea of a matchmaker, but now she was scared at how much she wanted it.

This process would streamline her entire dating life, and in some ways distribute the burden of finding The One. Less mental work. Less second-guessing. Higher probability of success.

"Okay, I'm going to blot my face before the buses arrive," Raven said, blowing a kiss and heading to the door. "Thanks for the latte."

Once alone, Gwen completed her prep for her first class of the day, an elective on career and life management. She'd been a high-strung student who'd have benefited from a bit of guidance and reassurance. So when the school district added this course, Gwen jumped at the chance to teach it on top of her English classes.

As the minutes passed, the hallways grew louder with junior high kids talking about their weekends and the school day ahead. The bell rang, and she stood up to let her students in.

"Good morning. Good morning," she said.

Some of the teens who were still trying to coax themselves awake ignored her greeting, while others waved.

After the second bell sounded and everyone was seated and quiet, Gwen said, "All right, we have a full schedule today. We're continuing our month of career profiles. This morning, we have two presenters because of the pep rally on Friday—"

"Does that mean we don't have to do journal entries today?" a student with glasses and curls dyed green asked.

"Yes, it means you won't have to do—"

A burst of excited chatter swept across the class.

"Okay, settle down. You'd think I make you draw blood for ink," Gwen said, laughing as she turned to write on the whiteboard. "Our first guest, Tim O'Hara, is a food blogger. And our second guest will be my brother, Duncan Gilmore, who will talk about what it's like to be a boxer and own a gym."

Gwen caught movement in her peripheral and turned to look out the small window of her door. "And it seems Mr. O'Hara is right on time. Give us one moment."

She exited her classroom and introduced herself to the writer. He was a lanky guy with thinning hair and a coat that sat heavily on his shoulders.

"You have fifteen minutes to talk, and then the class will have five minutes to ask you questions," she said.

The food blogger nodded but then took an obvious swallow before asking, "Are they mean?"

Gwen's eyebrows shot upward. "The students? No, they're good kids."

His question led her to read the sweat peppering his forehead differently.

"Mr. O'Hara," Gwen said gently, "they're very excited to hear about your work. They've enjoyed all of the previous speakers and have had the utmost respect for them. You'll do brilliantly."

The man rubbed his palms against the front of his khaki pants. "Okay, I'm ready."

He was, in fact, not ready because the moment he got in front of the thirteen-year-olds, he froze. When he eventually found his voice, it wobbled and stumbled across sentences. It was a relief then for everyone when the presentation came to a sputtering end several minutes later.

Her brother, Duncan, arrived shortly after, wearing an ugly costume mask for some reason.

"Why do you have that on?" Gwen asked her brother when she went outside the classroom to greet him. "Who is that?"

Duncan removed the mask and grinned. "Muhammad Ali. Thought it might enhance my presentation."

"Well, it's horrifying. And looks nothing like him," Gwen said before ushering her brother into the room.

Unlike the previous presenter, her brother was charismatic and natural in front of the students. Even with the questionable gimmick of the mask, he managed to sound sincere.

The question period mainly consisted of the kids asking Duncan about fight techniques and boxing match stories. When the bell rang, the students scattered, barely staying long enough to tuck in their chairs.

"Remember, if you need more time for the project or

want to adjust the assignment, come talk to me," Gwen shouted after them.

She expected to find her brother on his way out as well, but he was leisurely strolling the perimeter of her classroom.

"I appreciate you coming today," Gwen said as she settled behind her desk.

"Yeah, no problem," he said casually as he continued his little journey around her classroom.

He had a whole business to return to but had decided the fall decorations and posters on her wall were more important.

"What is it?" she asked.

"What? Nothing," he said, his voice pitched high as he turned to face her.

"What do you want?"

He shook his head and made protesting sounds before dropping the act and sliding into a tiny desk directly in front of hers. "Okay, yeah, I need a favor."

"I knew it."

"Before you reject it outright, have an open mind," he said.

"You sound like Mom."

"Well, you can be stubborn like her."

"Interesting tactic," she said, chucking her pen cap at him. "Insult the person you're about to ask a favor of."

"Fine, I'm sorry. I come to you as humbly as I possibly can to ask if you still have that pull-out couch?"

"Yes…" she said carefully.

Duncan smiled his oh-so-charming smile and asked, "Could Anthony move in with you for a few weeks?"

Anthony. Her brother's best friend and business partner. She didn't know him that well despite the men being friends for almost a decade. She could count on one hand the number of real conversations they'd had—all unremarkable.

"Ah, why?" she asked.

"His apartment's got some heating problems, so he's been staying at my place, but I'm pretty sure I'm killing him."

"I don't understand," she said.

"We're doing renos around the apartment, and we're fixing up the living room, and he's sleeping in there. And I'm kinda worried about all the paint fumes and dust."

"I'm sympathetic, I am, but…"

To Gwen, Anthony—Tony—was a sullen, moody type. He always seemed pissed about something, and that wasn't exactly the energy she was clamoring to be around.

"It would only be for a few weeks," he said quickly.

She hadn't lived with anyone since college, and that had been a disaster because of a stolen house slipper fiasco. Not even Eric, who she'd dated for almost three years, had spent more than a few consecutive days in her apartment.

"It'll be weird. I don't really know him," Gwen said.

"He's chill, I promise," Duncan said.

She knew she was going to say yes, even if she didn't want to. It was what older siblings did, but she wouldn't be happy about it.

"Okay, fine," Gwen said on a sigh.

Duncan banged the desk and stood up. "And this is why you're the best."

"On one condition," she said, lifting her hand to halt his compliments.

"What?"

"You burn that godforsaken mask."

Chapter Three

WHILE SITTING in the empty staff room at her brother's gym, Gwen waited for the impending interaction with Tony by scrolling through the Hearts Collide Matchmaking Service site on her phone. It was weirdly comforting, and it beat checking her application status every minute.

She put on her headphones and pressed play on the introduction video she could, at this point, recite.

"You're tired, aren't you?" the South Asian woman in the video asked. "Tired of scrolling and tapping and swiping for your next date only to realize the person you've decided to go out with is fundamentally *not* for you."

Gwen nodded like the lady might be able to see her.

"What if I could assure you that you'd find your perfect match and also stay together for the long haul?" the woman asked. "Well, at Hearts Collide, we'll be your guide through the dating world."

After filling out the application, Gwen believed that the agency knew almost everything about her. She provided information from her favorite snacks to which side of the bed she preferred.

"We use psychology, leading research on compatibility, and our own unique system that considers key factors to find your match. We find your soulmate. Someone who works for *you*."

Gwen's favorite part was up next, a montage of successfully matched couples with smiles that exposed all their teeth and eyes glassy from whatever neurotransmitter makes you feel in love.

She was so engrossed in the video that it took her a moment to realize she was no longer alone in the room.

Startled, she looked up and found her brother's best friend standing near the entrance of the staff room, studying her with dark eyes and a scowl.

"Didn't see you there," she said as she removed her headphones and stood up. "How's it going?"

His frown deepened.

For someone who would be on her couch for weeks, Gwen had the distinct feeling Tony wasn't happy to see her. She'd already accepted the different ways his presence in her home would inconvenience her, but it would've been nice to receive a bit of gratitude.

She waited for him to say something. Anything.

"You cut your hair," he said.

Okay, something other than *that*.

———

She had a perfect face.

Of course, Anthony already knew this, but finding his best friend's sister in the staff room hadn't been something he was prepared to confront today. The boldness of her features and her deep, dark skin demanded notice. A strong chin anchored her full lips, and the sharp slant of her cheekbones created a natural path up to her brown eyes. And one recent change emphasized all these details.

"You cut your hair," he said. The words sounded harsh and out of place. Perhaps he should've started with a hello.

Her hand shot to her short coils. "Months ago."

"It's… nice."

His attempt at a compliment landed as gracefully as a belly flop.

She smiled—or was it a grimace? "Thanks."

They stood there silent for a while until he asked, "Are you waiting for Duncan?"

"No, I'm here for you."

Something inside of him rolled and detonated, leaving him a bit lightheaded. He didn't know what to make of her words for several moments.

This crush he had on Gwen Gilmore had been nothing but a pain in his ass. He desperately wanted it to end. The initial spark of attraction could've been handled with a good fuck if she'd (1) shown even a bit of interest, (2) hadn't been in a relationship at the time, and (3) wasn't his best friend's sister.

Instead, his attraction had been left to stoke, to build to the point where he now was tongue-tied and awkward around her.

She rummaged through her purse before sliding a set of keys across the table toward him. "The big key is to enter the building, and the smaller one is for my apartment," she said.

Was he dreaming? Hallucinating? All signs were pointing to yes, but to be safe, he remained quiet and waited for her to explain further.

Her smile dropped. "He didn't tell you, did he?"

"Who? Tell me wh—"

"I thought I heard you guys in here," Duncan said jovially as he entered the staff room.

"You didn't tell him," Gwen said, planting her hands on her hips.

"Tell me what?"

"I didn't get the chance to."

"You could've texted him."

"Tell me what?" Anthony repeated, louder this time.

"We had a busy afternoon," Duncan told his sister.

"Hello!" Anthony shouted.

The siblings quietened, and Gwen gestured to her brother to speak.

"You're moving in with her," Duncan said.

"I'm sorry, what? Why?"

"Because if you don't, you're gonna inhale enough fumes to die on me. And I'm not getting saddled with the finances of this gym."

"It's not that bad," Anthony said.

But that was a lie.

His first night sleeping in his best friend's apartment had been a disaster. Yes, the paint and sawdust were unpleasant, but the place was also in that weird post-moved-in stage.

There were boxes everywhere, and the couch hadn't been delivered yet, so Anthony slept on an air mattress in the living room. But sometime during the night, the bed had popped, and in the morning, he woke up flush on the floor, freezing. The following night hadn't been much better.

"Come on, man. She has a pull-out couch," Duncan said.

Gwen's expression could be described as serviceably polite. She was definitely doing this as a favor to her brother.

"I promise I'm a good roommate," she said.

"Yeah, she snores, but you'll get used to it," Duncan said.

"Again, questionable tactic," Gwen replied through gritted teeth.

As the siblings exchanged light barbs, he tried to think of alternatives for his living situation because Duncan was right: he wouldn't last long on an air mattress in a dusty living room.

But he also couldn't stay with Gwen. He'd been able to manage his crush because they barely ever saw each other.

Plus, had he ever even lived with a woman? He'd dated a lot over the years, but he'd always had his own space. There was no reason for someone to settle in because the relationships never lasted very long. That was mostly due to his previous travel schedule and more recently the long hours involved in trying to get Spotlight up and running.

He could sleep at the gym instead! Why not? He'd shower in the locker room, get a nice little cot from Home Depot, and set it up in the office. And meals would be easy… Unless he wanted to use a stove. Also, the cleaners came early on Tuesdays, so he would have to get out of their way. Where would he store the cot during the day—

"Okay," Anthony said, and the siblings stopped talking.

"You'll move in?" Duncan asked.

He nodded, and no further fuss was made as Gwen gave him her address and phone number before leaving for the apartment they would share for several weeks.

He could barely focus during his last class of the day. If not for the familiarity of the music and the well-rehearsed routine, he didn't know if he could have provided a meaningful workout. But from the look of his smiling, sweaty clients, he'd done just that. And that relieved some of the tension in his body.

"Good job, coach!" a man in his sixties said, throwing Anthony a smile.

He received the older man's compliment with a small nod.

When Anthony had transitioned from professional fighter to gym instructor, he'd been nervous that his demeanor would scare off customers. He didn't know how to be charming and friendly in the way Duncan was. His friend would throw in jokes and cute asides during classes. But those who took Anthony's classes seemed to like him, so he was mostly over the insecurity.

After taking a quick shower in the locker room, he got dressed in fresh clothes and went through the gym's closing procedure. He knew he was stalling when he did the security check for the third time.

Eventually, he made it to Gwen's place with his belongings and enough takeout for two. He thought having seen her earlier that evening would lessen the blow, but he felt his chest tighten when she opened her apartment door and greeted him with a dimpled smile.

Short hair really did suit her.

She was on the phone but waved for him to enter. He removed his sneakers and remained rooted near the entrance, waiting for her to finish her call.

Gwen's apartment wasn't very big. The kitchen was to his left and the living room to the right. Neutral, muted furniture and appliances filled both spaces, and a neatly packed bookshelf hugged the right wall of the living room. The only thing that disrupted the order was the chirp of the smoke detector above.

When his eyes eventually found their way to Gwen, she was leaning over her kitchen counter. The slightly baggy loungewear set she'd changed into did nothing to camouflage the curves underneath. She moved like a dancer at a barre, mindlessly rising to the balls of her feet before lowering back down, the apple-red nail polish on her toes catching the light every time.

He stopped himself from studying her further and instead mentally fortified himself in the same way he had when he'd boxed professionally. But unlike those times long gone, he didn't feel at all ready and severely doubted his abilities to face the evening ahead.

———

He'd brought food.

It made the fact that Gwen was still wearing a bra this late into the evening worth it.

He stood near her entrance like a statue carved from brown marble, stoic and unimpressed. His eyes roamed her place, not staying in one spot for long. When she finally finished her call, she smiled at him, but she shouldn't have been surprised when he didn't return the expression.

She wondered, not for the first time, how this man could be friends with her perpetually amiable brother. Maybe his time in her home would help her figure that out.

"Your smoke detector needs a new battery," he said flatly.

Him and these non-greetings.

It took a few moments for the sound that had become white noise to come back into focus.

"Yes," she said, looking up at the ceiling and cursing the device for embarrassing her in front of company. "I'll get on that tomorrow."

There was nothing she could do about it right now.

"Well, welcome," she said as cordially as she could. "Let me give you a quick tour, and then we can eat."

She backed up, gesturing for him to step further into her home. When he did, he almost tripped over the package of her ex's belongings—speaking of men who were inconveniencing her. Eric had yet to reply to her request for a correct forwarding address.

"I'm so sorry," Gwen said, shoving the box more firmly into the corner before resuming her tour.

"This is the kitchen, and this is the living room," she said. "Congratulations, you've now seen eighty percent of my apartment."

Next, she showed him the linen closet where the clean towels and sheets were kept. She skipped her bedroom and headed straight to the tiny bathroom, where they stood uncomfortably close. It was mostly his fault. He took up a lot of room.

"The lock doesn't work, but you can use the drawer to keep the door closed," she said as she pulled it open to demonstrate. "Any questions? Concerns?"

She braced herself for a comment that pointed out other ways her housekeeping fell short.

"Thank you," he said. "For letting me stay here."

"It's no problem," she replied, hoping her face didn't betray her. "All I ask is that you clean up after yourself, restock what you finish, and, y'know, don't walk around naked."

The last point had to be made. He evidently had a nice body, strong and solid from his hours of training, but she had no desire to live through that awkward situation.

"Got it," he said, after clearing his throat.

"Perfect. Let's eat."

They served themselves food and settled in her living room. She thought it would be better if she didn't sit on his "bed," so she took the armchair to the left of the couch at a weird angle to the television.

They silently ate and watched the evening news for a while, but all Gwen could focus on was the persistent beeping of the useless smoke detector.

"How was work?" she asked in an attempt to drown out the sound and also be friendly.

Tony froze with his fork halfway to his mouth and turned to her with those very serious eyes and rogue spirally curls falling in his face, and said, "Good. You?"

His monosyllabic response deflated any desire in her to engage in chitchat. She'd spent all day trying to get reluctant teens to participate in class. There was no way she would try to force a grown man into small talk, so she simply replied as he had. "Good."

Maybe it was because her matchmaking application was so fresh in her mind, but Gwen couldn't help but reflect on how Tony was the opposite of what she was looking for in a partner.

Aloof and unreadable men may be the archetype for an enticing romantic lead in a movie, but for Gwen it just foreshadowed miscommunication, one-sided arguments, and an eventual explosive breakup.

They finished their respective meals with no further words.

As they cleared their dishes and tidied the kitchen, she said, "I should help you pull out the bed. I can never do it on my own."

"I'll manage," he said dully. "Thanks."

Of course he could manage. The man had strong arms and a broad back. She felt silly for even offering her help.

"All right, good night then," she said.

While she got ready for bed, mild resentment was her companion. Her evenings were a time when she could light a candle, croon in the shower, and do an overly involved skincare routine. But right now, she felt like she was in a communal locker room, trying to quickly scrub her body before someone demanded she "hurry the hell up."

When she finally made it to her room and under her covers, the damned squawking smoke detector kept her from even relaxing, never mind falling asleep.

How had she forgotten to replace the battery?

Knowing the type of luck she was having recently, her apartment would choose this day to catch on fire.

Not long after, Gwen heard Tony leave her apartment. She reached for her phone to text him, but put it back a moment later. It wasn't her business. Maybe he was going for a walk, taking a phone call, or heck, meeting someone.

He eventually returned, and she was still awake, trying to find comfort on the cool side of the pillow. There was movement like something heavy was being dragged across her floors, and Gwen sat up in bed, trying to decipher what was happening. Moments later, everything made sense when the beeping she'd become accustomed to just stopped.

Chapter Four

TO ANTHONY, there were very few things worth waking up before dawn for. Getting out of the apartment while Gwen was still asleep was one of those things.

He arrived at his empty studio and fussed over the neatly folded towels and boxing equipment. When he grew tired of that, he swept the floors in the staff room and cleaned out the fridge. All that busy work didn't even take him an hour, so he headed to the small office to do some paperwork he'd been neglecting.

This is where his best friend found him when he arrived.

"I thought I was opening today," Duncan said when he entered their shared working space, dumping his bags on a chair.

"You are," Anthony said, bracing himself for his friend's prodding questions. He had answers (lies) already planned out. But instead, Duncan started sniffing the air in front of him.

"You smell good," Duncan said, moving closer. "Like…"

"Lavender."

"Lavender," Duncan repeated, snapping his fingers. "My sister's, I'm guessing."

Of course it was Gwen's. He'd forgotten his shower gel at Duncan's place and had to use hers. It *did* smell nice, and he didn't care that he smelled like a garden, except it kept Gwen in the forefront of his mind, which wasn't what he wanted at all.

"How was last night?" his friend asked.

Anthony sighed.

"Ah, shit," Duncan said. "What happened?"

"Nothing. It was fine."

It had gone as well as it could have. If he furrowed his brows and set his chin at a certain angle, people usually didn't bother talking to him. That's how he liked it. But with Gwen, he'd felt a pull to make small talk about the weather and work or whatever else would've given him the opportunity to look at her. Thankfully, he'd resisted the impulse.

A knock sounded at the door, and one of the trainers popped her head in the office. "A Milo is here to see you guys."

"Oh, send him in," Duncan said.

Anthony looked up at his friend. "Who?"

"The social media manager," Duncan replied as he got spare seats from the corner of the room to make the office look more office-y.

Right.

The two of them were looking to increase their membership sign-ups with a strategy they'd built during a consultation with the popular public relations agency, BAX, several weeks ago.

They'd narrowed down the possible causes for their stalling business to a lack of public awareness and a months-long construction job that had impeded the usual flow to their complex.

Their instinct had been to buy ad space on the radio or something, but the agency had suggested they invest in building a cohesive and consistent brand online instead. It was supposed to target people most likely to sign up.

When Milo entered their office, Anthony noted he looked like the sort of guy who did this job. He wore glasses and had floppy hair and greeted them with strong handshakes and compliments about their studio.

"I'll be here a few times during the week," Milo said energetically. "To get footage, take pictures, and go over editorial calendars for the month. Today, I'll follow you guys around and collect some behind-the-scenes B-roll footage we can repurpose."

"All right then. Let's do it," Duncan said.

Milo turned the cramped space of their office into a makeshift set in a matter of minutes, with a ring light and two recording devices, a camera set on a tripod, and a smartphone in his hand.

"I like the idea of capturing the business side of the boxing studio," Milo said. "So, Anthony, get behind the desk and act like you're working on something."

Duncan had retreated out of frame and gave Anthony two thumbs-up like he was some stage dad.

"Act natural. Like I'm not even here," Milo whispered as he slowly prowled around the front of the desk with his camera.

Anthony looked down at the paperwork before him, feeling anything but natural as he scribbled down some figures and studied the pages. It was unnerving how close Milo got. Anthony knew his acne scars were on full display, but this was for the good of the studio, so he bore it. The social aspect of running a business had never come naturally to him. He'd resisted a lot of the social media stuff and gimmicky things that Duncan had previously encouraged. But it was a new day, and he was willing to get out of his comfort zone. To a point.

"This is great stuff," Milo said as he straightened and studied the footage he'd recorded.

Anthony stood up and said, "So we're done here?"

"For now," Milo said before he began to sniff the air. "It smells good in here. Floral?"

Anthony should've known then that the comment was a sign of things to come.

His body chemistry must have made the soap more potent somehow because he couldn't be in a room with someone without it coming up. And every time a person mentioned it, it messed up his plan to keep Gwen off his mind.

He didn't have a class to teach until the afternoon, so he couldn't even sweat off the fragrance. But during his short lunch break, he headed to the nearest drugstore and quickly picked out a random unscented soap.

The remainder of his day unfolded as expected, but instead of heading home immediately at the end of the day, he loitered around the studio as he had in the morning. By the time he got to Gwen's place, it was almost eleven at night.

He made sure to tread lightly when he entered the apartment. And as he'd hoped, she was already home and in her room fast asleep. He'd officially survived his first day living with Gwen.

Tomorrow he'd do it all again.

———

Gwen received the news that Hearts Collide Matchmaking Agency had accepted her application while she was in a staff meeting two days ago. She'd nearly knocked over her tea and made a sound that had elicited a concerned look from Raven. The quick response had been unexpected; she'd been certain she'd have to wait for weeks or months.

She hadn't felt nervous about the face-to-face consultation, but as she rode the elevator up to the agency's headquarters, a feeling settled in the pit of her stomach. The doors opened with a swoosh, and she was met with a sleek office that resembled a sterile science lab.

Gwen didn't know what she'd expected. Murals of Cupid and Aphrodite, maybe? But from what she could see, it was easy to assume her memory would be wiped upon departure.

The woman behind the front desk wore a crisp white button-down with a name tag, and the moment Gwen stepped forward, she turned away from her work on the computer and smiled.

"Gwendolyn Gilmore here for a meeting with Mary Neilson."

"Yes!" the receptionist, Sara, said, shooting up from her seat. "Welcome." She pulled a tablet from somewhere under the table and handed it to Gwen. "I'll get you to fill this out."

Gwen felt all she'd been doing was filling out documents, but she took the device and found a place to sit in the waiting room. Unlike the application and questionnaires she'd completed, this form only took a couple of minutes to get through. Once she returned to the desk, Sara led her through the building to an empty office.

"Take a seat," the receptionist said, gesturing to the chair designed as more of a visual piece than actual functional furniture. "Would you like something to drink?

Water, tea, coffee, hot chocolate, orange juice, passion fruit juice, pop…"

"You got any whiskey?" Gwen asked, laughing.

"Sure, we have Jack Daniels, Crown Royal—"

"Oh, I was kidding," Gwen said. "I'll have regular water."

"In a glass is okay?" Sara asked.

"Yes, thank you."

"What about a straw?"

"Sure."

"Would you like a lemon slice?"

"Why not."

"Ice?"

Jesus.

"You know what? Surprise me," Gwen said.

The receptionist nodded and left, and Gwen felt at least more at peace about siphoning money from her would-be vacation fund for this service. If they were this meticulous about their drinks menu, then hopefully they'd be the same with their roster of men.

While she waited, she scrolled through her phone, answering a couple of quick emails and replying to a text Tony had sent asking if she needed anything from the grocery store.

It had been days since Gwen had seen Tony with her two eyes. If she didn't find evidence of his existence throughout her home—extra towel in the bathroom, missing newspapers, and depleted peanut butter—she wouldn't even know he was there at all.

When she arrived home from work, he'd still be at the gym. She'd do some marking before eating dinner in front of the TV. He always returned when she was already in bed. His presence, as it turned out, was not as inconvenient as she'd anticipated.

The doors to the matchmaker's office opened, and Mary, a petite Black woman with a sharp blonde bob, appeared wearing a well-tailored all-white suit.

Mary spotted her and broke out into a big grin. "Oh my God. How are you?"

The vibrancy of the greeting took Gwen aback. "I'm good, thanks. I'm excited to be here."

"And *I'm* excited to find you the love of your life!" Mary said as she took quick little steps toward the desk Gwen was seated in front of.

The woman's warm energy was in stark contrast to everything in their surroundings, and it put Gwen at ease.

Before Mary could begin the meeting, a knock sounded at the door.

"Please come in, Sara," Mary said as the receptionist entered the room with Gwen's water and its accouterments on a tray.

"So, you're a teacher," Mary said once Gwen had her elaborate water in hand.

"I am."

"You're thirty-one, have a Master's in English Education, you play the piano…" Mary trailed in and out of sentences as she read the contents of Gwen's application from a screen. "You've never been married. No kids…"

Gwen kept nodding to affirm.

"Why don't you think it's worked out for you thus far?" Mary asked, peering over her cat-eye reading glasses. "Why are you single?

"I don't think it hasn't worked out. I was in a long-term relationship, but he wanted to move out east, and I wanted to stay right here. So we broke up."

Well, it was a little more complicated than that. Eric had thought they'd grown too comfortable.

"A slow march towards the suburbs, children, and death," he'd said.

But that's what they'd planned. With a few all-inclusive vacations sprinkled in, of course. That's what she thought they'd both wanted.

However, the moment she realized their visions for their future didn't align, it wasn't hard to let go. She hadn't wanted to spend years trying to make it work, only to find herself bitter and resentful. She'd seen that scenario play out between her parents when she was growing up.

"And you decided to try matchmaking because?" Mary asked.

"I realized I didn't feel like navigating a dating scene that can be unserious and slow-moving," Gwen said.

Her love life seemed like the last piece of the puzzle. She had a good, stable career, supportive friends and family, and a solid social life. All she needed to do was nail down this relationship thing, and she'd be set.

Mary's smile, which had not dimmed the entire time, seemed to grow wider somehow. And it was hard for Gwen not to take pride in seemingly acing the question.

"Perfect. So, if you could pick one quality for your future partner to possess, what would it be?" Mary asked.

One? Gwen had spent too many hours poring over the forms to narrow her preferences to one single thing.

"This isn't a trick question," Mary said, perhaps sensing her panic.

Gwen took a moment to think, discarding words that made her sound like a control freak before saying, "Kind. I want someone who is a good person."

The woman in charge of her love life quickly typed something on the screen of her device before saying, "I see you've picked the bronze package. That means we take all the information you've provided about yourself and find men already in our extensive database who are at least fifty percent compatible with you."

Gwen nodded.

"We'll send you a small batch of candidate profiles each week. You can choose to meet with none or all of them," Mary said, sliding her tablet over to Gwen. "And just for fun, here's a sneak peek of your first group."

Gwen studied the screen. Real men with commonalities beyond the fickle ones expressed in 300 characters.

The last bits of anxiety that Gwen had been holding in her body left her through an invisible sieve, and it was her turn to smile big and wide.

———

A few days were all Anthony needed to feel comfortable with his new living situation. The schedule wasn't the most desirable, but he could deal with long days and short nights because it was temporary. If in his pro boxing days, he'd survived brutal training sessions and flavorless, monotonous meals, surely he could make it through this.

When he entered the apartment on Friday night, he was ready to relish in the accomplishment of making it through a full week under Gwen's roof. However, a quick scan around the room told him she wasn't home yet.

The numerous bags she typically left propped up against the small entryway table weren't there, the hallway lights she usually left on for him were off, and her bedroom door was wide open.

Of course, his brain went in several directions. Stuck in a ditch somewhere with no cell service was one of the more immediate and extreme thoughts. But the more logical explanation was that it was the start of a weekend, and she was grown. She was most likely out with friends or something.

He proceeded with his typical nightly routine and got in the shower to wash off the day's sweat and dirt. He let the hot water ease his sore muscles and relax his mind.

With a towel around his waist, he stepped in front of the bathroom mirror to see what affirmation Gwen had stuck on the mirror today.

"Bit by bit," he read the affirmation out loud. He could picture her standing there in the morning, chanting it to herself.

Despite zero face-to-face interaction, Anthony had still managed to discover a couple of Gwen's habits. The affirmations on the mirror thing was one, and the way she inexplicably abandoned full cups of tea on the kitchen counter and in the living room was another.

Once he got dressed, he found something to eat and scarfed it down while standing at the counter. By the time he'd flossed and brushed his teeth, it was twenty minutes before midnight, and Gwen had still not arrived.

Unfurling his bed, he lay there with his eyes closed, hoping the gentle traffic and buzzing refrigerator would lull him to sleep. He had places to be tomorrow. But less than a minute later, he sat up in his bed and reached for a book at random on Gwen's nearby shelf.

Using the light from the hallway, Anthony flipped through an illustration-heavy coffee table book on the history of travel. Every so often, he'd pause to identify a sound coming from the hallway outside. Finally, a few minutes after midnight, keys jangled at the door.

Tossing the book off to the side, Anthony slid back under the covers just as Gwen entered her home. She barely made a sound as she removed her shoes and disappeared into her room.

Cool. So she wasn't catching hypothermia at the side of the road.

He felt a bit ridiculous that he'd stayed up, but something inside him relaxed, and he was able to fall into a deep sleep almost immediately.

———

Gwen woke up energized despite coming home later than she'd intended. She'd had her first date with a guy from Hearts Collide's database and was coasting on some sort of high. Miguel was most likely not The One, but knowing that they were compatible at a fundamental level made the experience more enjoyable than a regular date.

Grabbing her phone from her nightstand, Gwen logged onto her online profile to complete the required post-date survey. It was confidential and was supposed to refine the matchmaking formula that made the matches.

On a scale from 1-10, how would you rate the date (the activity, not the person):

Miguel had taken her to an indoor botanical garden early in the evening. The lush, vibrant plants and flowers were as stunning as their names were difficult. They'd laughed every time the other took a shot at pronouncing the Latinized words.

She placed a 9 in the empty field underneath the question.

Describe your feelings during the date:

She'd thought Miguel was a really nice guy. According to the agency's calculations, they were 62% compatible, and she believed it. They had all sorts of things in common.

However, at several points throughout the evening, she'd felt like she was speaking to a colleague. She didn't know if they had any real chemistry. His flirty comments laced with sexual innuendo had not inspired a spark or a single butterfly.

Gwen stopped typing and looked at the ceiling. When was the last time she'd masturbated? The abrupt thought and subsequent answer—too long ago—had her reaching inside the nightstand for her vibrator.

Settling on her back, she slid the device under her pajama pants and turned it on. The hum kickstarted a familiar tingle that raced from the base of her stomach to the tips of her toes. Her breathing soon quickened, and she slipped her hand under her shirt to take hold of her nipple in a firm pinch.

Her thoughts roamed through different sexy scenarios, mostly a faceless man fucking her, and the ascent toward bliss accelerated. She came while fisting her sheets and didn't curtail her moans.

Once her heart rate settled, she slid out of bed and shuffled to the bathroom, where she washed her hands and vibrator before heading to the kitchen for breakfast. But with her eyes glued to her phone, she didn't notice Tony until she was right in front of him.

She looked up, and before her brain could tell her body all was well, she screamed and launched her fist at his face.

"Oh my God," Gwen shouted. "I'm so sorry."

"I-it's fine," Tony said while moving his jaw around.

"I didn't know you were home. You're never home," she said. It sounded like an accusation, a complaint of a fed-up wife.

"I woke up late," he said, almost sounding embarrassed. "I'm sorry, I didn't mean to scare you."

She opened her freezer and grabbed a bag of peas. "Here."

"It's fine," he said.

"You're telling me my hand is throbbing, and you can't feel a thing?" she asked, placing the frozen bag on her knuckles instead.

"You hurt yourself," Tony said, his frown deepening somehow.

"Nothing's broken." She thrust her hand out and wiggled her fingers. "But I'd like to inform you that your face is a damn brick."

The crease between his brows softened slightly, and she couldn't be certain, but she thought he might be amused.

"For the record, I do feel it," he said, taking the peas from her and slapping it on his jaw.

"You were about to give me a complex about my right jab," she said, only sort of joking.

"I guess I'm used to taking hits."

Gwen's eyes drifted to Tony's nose. It had clearly been broken several times. It was crooked and thick around the bridge. There was no subtlety or elegance about it either, but it suited him and gave him a face that you wanted to study.

As she moved around him to turn on the kettle, she caught her reflection in the microwave and stilled.

Almost half of the top buttons of her pajama shirt were unfastened, and her boobs were dangerously close to giving a morning salutation. She quickly corrected the malfunction, but her cheeks grew hot as it dawned on her that Tony had been in the apartment while she'd been masturbating in her room with shameless abandon.

That wouldn't be such a big deal, but her home had three downsides: the WiFi was spotty, the water pressure was inconsistent, and *the walls were thin*.

"I'm heading out," Tony said over the sound of the whistling kettle.

She spared him a look over her shoulder. If he'd indeed

heard her, she couldn't tell by his expression. "Okay, see you."

Once the door closed behind him, Gwen splayed her upper body across the counter. She had papers to mark and an abandoned survey to complete, but for several minutes, she fantasized about crawling under a human-sized rock.

Chapter Five

WHAT WAS it about retail store parking lots that brought out the worst in people?

Anthony had just finished watching two patrons argue over a shopping cart when a man in an SUV pulled up trying to squeeze into the parking space right next to Anthony's. The car clearly wouldn't fit, but still, the man inched forward as if faith would somehow change the dimensions of the space. Anthony rolled down his window, ready to tell the driver to give up, but the guy seemed to realize his folly and left to find a more appropriate spot.

With the crisis averted, Anthony leaned forward against his steering wheel and scanned the hoard of people entering and exiting the store, and spotted the reason for his presence moving nimbly through the crowd toward Anthony's truck.

Old Man Enoch was his childhood neighbor, and one of the biggest influences on his life. He was short and round with a mustache that had sat on his upper lip for all the decades Anthony had known him. His once-small Afro had disappeared and been replaced with a shiny brown head.

"Got it," Enoch said triumphantly once he entered the truck with a plastic bag in hand. "Let's go."

"Are you sure you want to do this?" Anthony asked as he backed out of the space.

"Of course I'm sure. I can't ignore cheating."

Since retiring, Enoch had occupied his time with all kinds of projects and activities. For the past five years, he'd entered the Great Giant Pumpkin Weigh-off. It was a serious competition for those who participated, and it wasn't for the faint of heart.

If you wanted to go toe-to-toe with the pros, you had to start a year before, tilling and nurturing the ground you planned to raise a giant vegetable in. A monetary reward and trophy were waiting for the contestant with the heaviest pumpkin.

So understandably, people got upset when a rumor started circulating that the three-year reigning champion, Jeremy, had been pumping his pumpkins with water to give himself an edge.

The judges didn't take the accusation seriously, however, so a small collective of previous and current Great Giant Pumpkin Weigh-off participants had made it their mission to catch the cheat in the act by staking out in Jeremy's neighborhood.

Was it legal?

Anthony wasn't sure.

Was he doing it anyway?

Yeah, because he'd do anything for the old man.

"I'm getting Katherine that trip to Jamaica," Enoch said of his wife.

Anthony followed the GPS to their destination while

Enoch read the instructions for his newly purchased binoculars.

"There it is," Enoch said once they arrived in Jeremy's neighborhood. He pointed to a beige house with fall decorations at the front. "Try to get a spot with a view of the backyard."

Anthony circled the block.

"Right here, right here," Enoch said as Anthony moved to park on the side of the quiet road. There was a giant pumpkin in the backyard, all right. However, only the top of it was visible from their vantage point.

"Okay, we just sit here and?"

"And wait," Enoch said as he reclined his seat. "Hours if we have to. We have enough water and snacks. We can stay till the sun sets and the crickets start—"

"An hour and a half is all I got," Anthony said.

"That works too."

Anthony wasn't entirely sure what he was waiting to see, but he settled into his seat and embraced the janky stakeout.

"Katherine's been wondering when you're coming to pick up the lamps and table," Enoch said after some time.

"Ah, forgot about that," Anthony said, rubbing his head.

The older couple were getting rid of some of their furniture, and they'd offered Anthony a few pieces.

"I'll pick it up sometime next month. I'm not staying at my apartment right now."

Enoch gave him a sidelong look. "Do I need to worry?"

"Nah, I'm good. They're fixing some heating issues."

"Where you living now?" Enoch asked.

"With Duncan's sister."

His mind returned to that very morning in Gwen's

kitchen. He'd planned to leave early like usual, but he'd forgotten to set his alarm.

On weekends he had off, he never bothered with an alarm. But this wasn't a regular weekend. He was living with Gwen. When he'd finally woken up and realized his mistake, he'd prepared himself for the possibility that she'd wake up before he had the chance to leave.

What he hadn't anticipated was hearing Gwen in her room pleasuring herself.

He'd initially thought he was imagining things, but the high-pitched, breathy moans were undeniable. If he hadn't been holding onto the counter at that moment, he wouldn't have remained upright. His heartbeat had been in his throat, and his body had felt like he'd landed on the surface of the sun.

She'd entered the kitchen with rumpled pajamas and a punch, but her blow couldn't dislodge the image of her writhing on her bed from his mind.

"You staying there for free?" Enoch asked, pulling Anthony from his thoughts.

"Yeah, just pitching in with groceries."

"Good. Good. Well, if anything changes, you know who to call."

There was no need to inconvenience more people. His apartment would be fixed in no time. He'd return to knowing Gwen in passing, and questions like "Do her toes curl when she comes?" would recede into the background.

"Oh, almost forgot," Enoch said as he dug into the plastic bag and pulled out a pack of candy. "I got M&M's."

As the old man poured multi-colored chocolates into Anthony's outstretched hand, there was a knock on the rear window of his truck.

"Ah, dammit," Enoch said as they both looked back.

A white man in his fifties was making his way around Anthony's vehicle to the passenger side.

"Who's that?" Anthony asked.

"It's Jeremy. Act cool," Enoch said as he rolled down the window.

Easy. They were only just spying on the man.

"Oh, well, hello there, Jeremy," Enoch said. "What are you doing here?"

"Nice try, Enoch. I know why you're here," Jeremy said, leaning forward to take a look inside the truck. "You're not the first to show up."

"I don't know what you're talking about. I'm house shopping with my godson."

God, let him not get pulled into this. He was only the driver.

"With binoculars?" Jeremy asked, gesturing to the instrument.

"We're going bird-watching afterward."

"Don't they do that little trip down south around this time of year?" Jeremy asked.

"Some of them. Not all," Enoch replied.

"Really? Which ones stay exactly?"

Enoch shrugged. "That's what we're gonna find out."

Jeremy laughed loudly. "Why can't you admit you're threatened by me? You can't win on your own merit, so you have to discredit mine."

"Merit is such an interesting word, isn't it?" Enoch said.

"If it would ease your mind, I can give you a tour of my backyard."

"No need. As I said, we're house shopping."

"Well then, have fun."

The champion sauntered off toward his home, and Anthony said, "House hunting and bird-watching?"

"It was the best I could do under pressure," Enoch said defensively.

"What now?"

"Our cover's blown. Doubt he'll do anything today. But just wait," Enoch said, his voice growing louder as he spoke. "The chickens will come home to roost. Might not be this year. It might not even be next year. But eventually, Jeremy Blush will be exposed for the fraud he is and be knocked down a few pegs."

"Okay, cool. In the meantime, you wanna grab some lunch?" Anthony asked.

"Oh, yes," Enoch said, quickly straightening his seat. "Let's get those teriyaki burgers we got last time."

———

Gwen's second date through the agency was with a web developer named Nelson. He had a thick beard and a real smooth silky voice that had her leaning in when he spoke. They were 60% compatible and spent a large chunk of time talking about their respective global travels.

Then there was the documentary filmmaker, Malik. She'd worn gold hoops and a black turtleneck, and he'd told her she looked like '90s Nia Long. The compliment alone almost made her rate the date higher than she ultimately did.

The physical education teacher, Carl, was sweet and not dissimilar to a golden retriever. He gave her high-fives and said, "Right on!" whenever she made a statement. Like:

"I skied for the first time three years ago."
"Right on!"

"I can't really sit through an entire Christopher Nolan movie."

"Right on!"

"I don't think we're going to work."

"Right on!"

While she was still enthused and committed to the process, it was an exhausting schedule. She'd usually go out on a date after work, and sometimes it would end late. Then she'd have to do her marking and hopefully remember to plug in her phone to charge before passing out.

It was no wonder then, while eating lunch in the staff lounge one day, Raven said, "You look rough, babe."

The energy in the room was mostly sedate as the other school employees pretended to be interested in the football coach's dramatization of a decades-old *Saturday Night Live* sketch.

"I've been on a date every day this week," Gwen said as she picked out the onions from her Italian sub.

"Jesus. Why no breaks?" Raven asked, pulling out a tube of concealer from her purse and applying and blending some under Gwen's eyes.

"I set it up like that. I thought it would be more efficient," Gwen said.

"It sounds like a bad part-time job."

"But it's getting me closer to my perfect match," Gwen said. "That's what matters."

"When's your next one?" Raven asked.

"Tonight. It's a second date with…" Gwen quickly opened her calendar on her phone. "Nelson. He's a computer person of some kind."

"What are you guys doing?"

"He's coming over for dinner."

Raven's eyebrows shot upward. "At your apartment?"

"Yeah, I thought it would be a nice change of pace," Gwen said, showing her friend a picture of the table she'd set up that morning. "And he doesn't seem like a creep, so."

She planned on ordering food from one of her favorite restaurants and picking up fresh flowers from the grocery store.

"It'll be real chill, and we'll be done before Tony gets back—"

"Tony? Who the hell is Tony?" Raven asked.

"I didn't tell you about my temporary roomie?"

"Um, no. When did this happen?"

"It's not a big deal. He's my brother's business partner, and he's staying with me for a few weeks until his apartment problems get fixed."

Raven looked wistfully into the distance. "I've always wondered what it would be like to have a roommate."

"Girl, you've had roommates."

"No, I've lived with boyfriends. It's different," Raven said.

"You romanticize the weirdest shit. I promise you we're not painting each other's nails and watching Shonda Rhimes shows."

"So it's going badly?"

"No, it's going well. Though I *did* accidentally punch him in the face."

"Oh my God," Raven said sharply. "What?"

"Also, I'm pretty sure he heard me masturbating in my room."

"Wow, incredible. In a span of a few seconds, you've made the roommate thing completely unappealing."

"But other than those incidents, it's been good because

we don't interact with each other. He's not the chatty type."

"Oh?"

"Yeah, he's a bit…" Gwen scrunched her face trying to imitate Tony.

"Angry?"

"No, aloof. Grumpy."

Gwen had never in her life seen someone maintain a frown for that long, and she spent her working days with moody teens.

She was itching to smooth the lines in between Tony's brows with her thumb. She suspected that he'd be sort of be handsome if he could just relax his face a bit. He had these hypnotically dark eyes and skin the color of polished mahogany. And enviable lashes and a wide mouth that—

"You good?" her friend asked.

"What?"

"You went somewhere for a second," Raven said.

"Yeah," Gwen said, a little embarrassed that she'd been caught considering Tony's alleged handsomeness. "I just remembered I need to text Nelson to confirm our date."

———

It was 12:34 p.m. when Anthony got the text.

Gwen: Dinner's at 7 p.m. Don't be late ;)

A photo of Gwen's kitchen bar, set for a fancy meal, accompanied the message.

It wasn't unusual for them to text, but the topics were limited to garbage removal or money owed by the other for groceries.

This message, then, was not meant for him.

Anthony: Hey, I think you texted the wrong person.

He waited for the little speech bubble on her end to pop up, but all he saw was that his text had been delivered.

"Have you heard anything I've said?" Duncan asked.

Anthony looked over at his best friend where he was jumping up and down in an attempt to stay warm. They stood outside waiting for their turn with the photographer taking their new masthead photos for the website.

Anthony didn't see a problem with the ones they had now, but their social media manager insisted they needed pictures that looked more inviting and less like a team that would pummel their clients.

"Yeah, yeah. 'We need to find time to talk about programming,'" Anthony repeated the last words he heard his friend say.

Duncan looked down at the phone Anthony held in a grip. "Everything good?"

"Yeah," Anthony said, slipping the phone into his joggers.

Duncan squinted and continued to study him. "You sure—"

A text came through, and Anthony quickly checked it.

It wasn't from Gwen.

Anthony looked back up to find Duncan studying him.

"What?" Anthony asked, shifting uncomfortably as his friend ignored his question and continued to stare.

After a moment, Duncan softly said, "Holy shit." His mouth hinged open. "It's a woman."

"What? No," Anthony said roughly.

"Nah. Don't lie to me, man. I see it," Duncan said.

His best friend had fallen in love and now thought himself an expert on the topic. He'd become evangelical about the whole thing.

"So who is she?" Duncan probed.

There was no way he was talking to Duncan about Gwen. Never mind that there wasn't anything *to* talk about.

"Nobody."

"There's definitely somebody."

"Your evidence?" Anthony asked.

"That phone you're clutching like it's your life source."

"Listen. She—" Anthony froze, realizing he'd slipped up.

"Ha!" Duncan said, pointing at him. "I knew it!"

"Aye, chill."

He'd given Duncan an inch; he wouldn't let it go now.

"Fine, you don't have to talk about it with me. Yet," he said with a smile that was too big.

It was futile to argue with his friend, and he didn't get a chance anyway because the photographer shouted, "Okay, let's get the two owners in a picture together."

They posed in front of the frosted window of the business.

"We'll start with a smiling one," the photographer said.

"That's when you lift the corners of your mouth," Duncan whispered.

Anthony bared his teeth at his friend before turning back to face the camera.

They took a few more photos that had him feeling like it was Picture Day in elementary school, and through all of it, he kept his ear alert to any incoming messages.

None came.

He taught two classes, took a shower, completed admin work, and solved a customer service problem all by the time the clock struck 6:30. And Gwen still hadn't texted back.

Anthony's day was technically done besides a meeting he and Duncan were supposed to have in fifteen minutes.

He texted his friend to postpone their conversation till tomorrow before collecting his duffle bag and heading toward the exit.

Anthony questioned his actions with every mile he drew closer to Gwen's apartment. He was driving all this way to confirm what he already knew. He'd walk into her apartment, she'd be having dinner with someone else, and he'd have to make himself scarce for the evening.

The moment he stepped off the elevator on Gwen's floor, he heard a piercing ringing that only got louder as he neared her door.

When he opened it, he found her place in a state of chaos. Smoke bloomed from the oven, empty takeout containers littered the countertops, and Gwen, in a very pretty sweater dress, waved the morning newspaper underneath the wailing smoke detector.

"Hey, how's it going?" she said lightly.

Chapter Six

THE PERSISTENT WAILING of the smoke detector knocked Anthony out of his shock, and he quickly moved to the living room to slide the large windows open. The gush of cold air stopped the noise almost immediately.

"You okay?" he asked Gwen, tempering the urge to draw nearer.

"Yeah, I was trying to keep buttered bread warm in the oven. I guess it's a good thing you changed the battery for this thing when you did," she said with a laugh.

She seemed to think nothing of his presence as she entered the kitchen, flitting around, dumping burnt bread in the bin, clearing the clutter off the counter, and rummaging through cabinets.

It wasn't until she was triumphantly holding up a corkscrew she'd extracted from a drawer that she froze and asked, "Are you here to pick up something?"

He imagined that was her nice way of asking why the hell he was there. It was a confirmation that the text hadn't been for him.

Tony cleared his throat. "Have you checked your phone recently?"

Gwen reached over for her cell that was charging on the counter. "No, it died on me in the middle of the day."

"I think you accidentally texted me," he said.

"Shit," she whispered as she studied the screen of her smartphone. "I've been so scatterbrained recently."

It seemed like equal parts an explanation for him and admonishment of herself.

She sent a series of texts before looking up and saying, "I'm sorry you came all this way. I meant to let you know not to come home till after eight, but the day got away from me, evidently."

"Nah, it's all good. I had some time," Tony said, backing toward the door. "I should leave before your guest arrives."

"Wait. If you still have time," she said, shortening the distance between them, "would you like to eat dinner with me?"

He looked at the decidedly romantic dining set up then back to her.

"I was expecting someone, but I just rescheduled since it would take him almost an hour to get here," she explained. "Now I have all this spaghetti and gazpacho from Sweet Bowl."

The smart move would be for him to refuse and head back to the studio. His polite decline was on the tip of his tongue, but he lost himself while looking at her and instead said, "Yeah, sure. I can stay."

"Perfect," she said brightly, handing him a ladle.

They served themselves and rejected the formal dining setup for the seats in the living room. Gwen didn't try to make conversation, unlike the first night when they'd last had dinner together. Instead, she put on that day's recording of *Cup of Joe*, a local morning talk show Anthony knew about only because one of the hosts was a fellow Riverside High School alum.

"Who in the audience takes fish oil capsules or daily multivitamins of some kind?" the woman presenter asked.

The camera panned to the crowd, where the majority clapped in response to her question.

"Well, there's a new supplement on the horizon that some of you might want to take. It's purported to make you less annoying," she said, elbowing the male co-host to the amusement of the studio audience.

The ensuing conversation was annoying. It was the type of babble Anthony could only stomach in small doses.

"Everything okay?" Gwen asked.

He looked at her for the first time since they'd sat down to eat.

"You made a little"—she huffed—"sound. Is it the food?"

He looked down at his nearly cleared-off plate and back to her. "No, the food's good. It's…" He couldn't exactly insult her taste in television, so he nodded toward the screen and said, "I went to high school with that guy."

"Hold up, you went to school with Aussie Bae?" she asked.

"Well, he went by Russell when I knew him."

"I didn't come up with the name, but I think it's the Thor thing he has going on."

"It's fake," Anthony said.

"What is?"

"The Australian accent."

"No, it's not," Gwen said. "He talks—"

"Trust me. He sounded like every white guy from the prairies, then switched it up halfway through high school."

"I can't believe it," Gwen said, looking back at the TV.

"I've watched this show for years. His accent is a staple as much as the blue and yellow set."

It was a grift that seemed to be working out for him too. Russell's early adoption of the schtick seemed to be the key to why he'd never been called out as a fraud during his broadcasting career. Either people who knew him back then assumed they had misremembered his original accent or, like Anthony, didn't see it as any of their business.

"How does he even maintain it?" Gwen asked.

"A seven-figure salary probably helps."

"Damn," Gwen said, turning to him. "You have to tell me more."

"I have nothing else to tell you about Aussie Bae. As you can probably guess, we didn't run in the same circles."

Anthony was sure Russell wouldn't even recognize him today.

"And what circles did you run in?" she asked.

"The ones that skipped classes mostly," he replied with a shrug.

"Huh."

"What?" Tony asked.

"No. Nothing. It's just I can picture that."

He raised his brows.

"That wasn't meant to be an insult. All I'm saying is if you told me you were a band geek or on the debate team, I'd have been a little shocked. But you being a bit of a rebel doesn't stretch my imagination."

Her attention returned to the morning show, where the hosts were introducing their next guest.

And for some reason, maybe because he wanted Gwen to look at him with the same fascination she was still staring at Russell with, he said, "I was a theater kid."

Gwen turned to him. "Fuck off."

"Senior year. I needed a few credits to graduate. I auditioned and got a minor part in *Man of La Mancha*."

One minor (non-speaking) role does not a theater kid make, but his admission made Gwen throw her head back and laugh. The dimple in her cheek appeared, and the sound of her laughter curled around him, tempting him to join in her mirth.

"Amazing," she said. "I guess everyone has talents or interests that defy people's perception of them."

"What's yours?" he asked.

"What?"

"Your talent or interest."

"Well, what's your perception of me?" she asked, placing her empty dishes on the side table.

He studied her for a moment. She'd removed her massive earrings and had tucked her feet underneath her on the chair. A whole bunch of adjectives came to mind, but he sifted through them until he landed on a few he was comfortable saying out loud.

"You're dependable, hard-working, and put together."

"You make me sound like a gently used Subaru," she said, laughing again. "Give me a second. Let me think."

After a moment of pensively studying the ceiling, Gwen meekly said, "I got something. But you have to promise not to tell anyone."

Her face had turned serious, and Anthony got nervous. He had no idea what to expect, but he nodded.

Gwen smoothed out the napkin on her lap, took a deep breath, and said, "I can burp the alphabet."

At first, Anthony thought he'd misheard her, but the playful glint in her eye told him differently.

She placed her hand on her chest and sniffled a little, and said, "You know when they say, with great power comes—"

"Fuck off," he said, a smile pressing the corners of his

mouth.

"It's true, I swear!" Gwen said, raising her open hand in the air.

"Let's hear it then."

"Oh, no. Only the forty people who were at Micky's Bar in summer of 2015 will ever get the privilege."

"How convenient," he said, standing up with his dishes to head to the kitchen.

"What is that? Reverse psychology?" she asked, following right behind him. "It won't work. Unless you're willing to bust out into song and dance, I'm not sharing my God-given talent."

He turned toward her. "I would, but"—he made a big show of stretching his triceps—"I'm feeling a little stiff and sore. As you know, I work out for a living, so—"

"How convenient," she said dryly.

There was that laugh again that wanted to emerge from his belly.

"I've got an apple galette from The Dutch Oven," Gwen said as she placed her dishes into the sink. "You want some?"

"Sure," he replied with little hesitation. He didn't particularly like dessert, but he unwisely wanted to prolong their interaction.

"There's also some ice cream in the freezer," she said.

Instead of returning to the living room to eat their dessert, Gwen sat at the bar, and Anthony stood against the counter. The sound of the forks hitting their plates filled the silence for a minute.

"Thanks for dinner," he said.

"No, thank _you_. There was a lot of food, and I'd have probably had to share it with Brenda."

"Brenda?" he asked.

"My neighbor. Big glasses, White hair, fabulous

caftans."

"Ah, yeah. I've seen her around," he said.

"She's a harmless gossip, but a gossip nonetheless," Gwen said before pointing her spoon at him. "Do you know she was the first person to find out Eric and I had broken up?"

This was the first time Gwen had mentioned her ex. Anthony met the guy once in passing. He'd been smiley and arrogant-looking in some stiff suit.

"To this day, I don't even know how she figured it out."

Anthony frowned. "Did she tell people?"

"No, but for once, it would've been helpful if she had. Notifying everyone that you're no longer in a relationship is the second worst thing about a breakup. Someone needs to come up with a service for that."

"Notice of *EX*-termination," Anthony said after a moment.

"Oh, that's clever!" she said with a laugh. "Draw up the papers. I'd invest in that business."

Anthony smiled a little. "I think I'm good with the one business for now."

"How's that going? The gym."

"Good," he said before adding, "We have a guy now. A social media manager."

"Oh, yeah. Duncan was telling me about that."

It was all jargon with Milo. "Brand voice" this, "SEO compliant content" that. Anthony was sure he looked like a robot failing to compute while Milo spoke to them.

Once he and Gwen finished their respective pie slices, he said, "I'll take care of the dishes."

"You sure?" she asked.

He nodded, taking her dessert plate.

"Okay, cool. You've eliminated a reason for me to procrastinate on my marking. I'll see you later."

"Good night," he said before she disappeared down the hallway.

The tension he'd been holding in his shoulders eased and was quickly replaced by a warmth that radiated from the center of his chest.

———

Sunday brunch was a Gilmore family tradition that occurred once a month.

It had been facilitated by a therapist a decade ago when her parents were still fooling themselves into thinking that they could live a harmonious life together.

For a long time, it was something Gwen dreaded. They were usually tense occasions—a Wild West cowboy duel where all that strung the minutes together were awkward silences and surface-level conversation. But since the divorce, Malcolm and Trudy Gilmore had made these occasions less grating.

"Is this enough?" Gwen asked her mother of the pitcher she'd been squeezing a combination of blood oranges and regular oranges into.

"Do one more of each," her mom said before turning back to the hash browns she was handling over the stove. "How's matchmaking going?"

Thirty-seven minutes. Her mom held off from asking her about her dating life for thirty-seven minutes. Which Gwen supposed she should applaud her for.

"Good. It's coming along nicely," she replied.

Her mom turned to face Gwen with her hands on her hips. "Baby, you have to give me more than that. Tell me about your last date."

Despite having one just last night at an art gallery with a pharmacist named Derrick, her head immediately went to the accidental dinner with Tony a few days ago. How, in two hours, her entire opinion of him had changed. It had been a surprisingly pleasant evening.

He'd smiled. Twice! They hadn't been full-blown smiles, mind you, but it was enough that she'd started anticipating the next one. She would have never known that Tony had a dry sense of humor and could be a bit playful.

"You're smiling," her mom said, waving her finger in Gwen's face. "There's someone, isn't there?"

Gwen schooled her features. "No, not yet."

"That smile looked very dreamy."

"God, I haven't met my soulmate yet. I've gone on a good number of dates that have ranged from mediocre to fantastic. But I promise not to get engaged without running it by you first."

"Aw. Remind me to leave you the fine china in my will," her mom said moments before her brother and his girlfriend, Retta, strolled through the front door.

Duncan balanced two boxes which undoubtedly held pastries from Retta's bakeshop.

They had met a little over a year ago, and they had fallen hard and fast. It seemed to surprise the people around them, mainly their parents, because Duncan had never been the one to do committed relationships. Gwen, however, knew the moment she saw her brother interacting with Retta that things were different.

"I like these," Gwen said of Retta's new glasses after they'd exchanged hugs.

"Oh," Duncan said, laughing. "You gotta tell her."

Retta sighed. "I slammed my face in pie and accidentally broke my old glasses."

Gwen laughed. "For fun or?"

"It was for a charity thing, and I forgot to remove

them," Retta said, shaking her head.

Duncan kissed the side of her mouth and whispered something in her ear that she chuckled at. Gwen smiled at the couple's interaction but spared them all the fawning she could've done over how adorable they were.

Polite conversation was shared as they all worked to set up the last bits of brunch. Gwen was in the kitchen placing the pastries Retta had brought on a decorative dish when her father arrived. Her smile dropped when she saw who was on his arm.

"Shit," she mumbled.

Her brother turned to her. "What? You mess things up already—" The teasing tone in his voice faded when he spotted what she had.

Their father and his new girlfriend hung on the threshold of the kitchen as if waiting for everyone to notice them.

Gwen and Duncan both looked at their mother chatting away with Retta.

"He told me about her," Duncan said.

"Me too, but I didn't think he'd show up with her."

She didn't begrudge her father for moving on. But to bring another woman into his ex-wife's house was asking for trouble.

"What do we do?" he asked.

"Tell him to get her out of here," Gwen whispered as she waved at her father with a stiff smile.

There was no way to enjoy egg souffle with people flinging obscenities over your head.

Before her brother could approach their dad, their mom looked up, perhaps sensing the anxiety emanating from her children.

Gwen held her breath, her grip tightening around the pastry box in her hand.

This was bad.

But her mother didn't even break a beat before standing up and saying, "Malcolm, you're finally here. And I see you've brought…"

"Abigail."

"Abigail," their mother repeated the name as if it was some foreign perfume she'd been recommended. "Come on in. The food is almost ready."

Gwen and Duncan shared a look.

"How?" Gwen whispered.

"Don't question it. Let's hope we get through this unscathed," Duncan said as he picked up a dish to take to the table.

Her father had obviously brought Abigail along to make some sort of statement. Whether it would remain implied or get loud was yet to be seen.

Gwen stayed on alert as everyone took their seats and served themselves. Mitigator was a familiar role for Gwen, one she'd unintentionally stepped into as child whenever her mom and dad fought. She kept glancing between her parents, looking for the crack in their otherwise pleasant expressions that would let her know if one of them was about to snap.

But as brunch unfolded, things stayed light, and Gwen's mom smiled, laughed, and even asked Abigail questions. And Gwen started to relax and enjoy her food and the company.

"I really love your silverware, Trudy," Abigail said partway through the meal.

"Malcolm got it for me for our fourteenth anniversary."

The way her mom said "fourteenth anniversary" in a clipped tone prompted Gwen to look over at her brother who'd similarly caught the cadence shift.

"They're beautiful," Abigail responded earnestly.

"Thank you."

Their dad took a hold of his girlfriend's hand on the table and said, "We'll get a similar set for the new place, then."

Her father's words settled around them like a soggy blanket, and her mom flatly asked, "You're moving in together?"

"Yeah, sometime in the near future," he responded casually before shoveling hash browns into his mouth.

In that moment, Gwen felt her heart rate pick up as the different ways the morning could devolve from there played out in her head.

She scrambled to come up with something to say to distract them all.

"Did I tell you that I think the principal at my school is stealing from the lost and found?" Gwen asked quickly.

Everyone turned to her.

"What? No way," her brother said with exaggerated enthusiasm.

She knew Duncan understood what she was trying to do and was aiding her in her efforts.

"Yeah, I saw him pick out expensive headphones from the bin the other day," Gwen said before recounting a slightly embellished story about her boss's petty thievery.

The tale had her intended effect, and tension was diverted and the conversation shifted to many other subjects before the food was mostly gone and everyone was full. Gwen's mother excused herself to the kitchen to prepare coffee to accompany Retta's pastries, and Gwen followed behind to help.

Her mom had a smile still pasted on in a sort of way that had Gwen a little worried that she might fling a plate across the room.

"Mom?"

The older woman stopped humming. "Yes, love?"

"You okay?" she asked.

Her mother turned to her and, through her teeth, said, "Just peachy."

That was obviously untrue.

"If you want, I can talk to Dad about bringing her," Gwen said.

"Don't be ridiculous. He doesn't have to run things by me anymore. We're divorced," she said, laughing. But it failed to come off as lighthearted as Gwen suspected her mom had intended.

Her parents' relationship had been the thing in Gwen's life that had caused her the most grief. And it was why she knew that finding someone compatible—really compatible—was important. Though she respected her parents, it scared her no end to think that she could be in their position, having wasted almost half her life with a person who wasn't meant for her.

And she didn't know if it was hubris, but she thought she could make a long-term relationship work. She could do it better than her parents because she knew the pitfalls and could anticipate the complications. All she needed was the right partner to give it a shot with.

———

Anthony had been reduced to observing time in terms of how long it had been since he last interacted with Gwen.

Current status: three days and fourteen hours.

It was an embarrassing reality to admit, that a couple of hours spent together at dinner could turn him into a pining fool. But he'd made a concerted effort to settle back into his original rhythm of living with Gwen.

However, that was easier said than done. He was still avoiding her in the mornings, but to Anthony's dismay, he was unable to relax enough to fall asleep unless Gwen was in the apartment at night. And unfortunately, she'd been coming home late almost every day.

Oh, he'd tried to sleep, even going so far as to count sheep.

But it didn't help. All that was left for him to do was bide his time each evening until Gwen got home safely. On the first night, he'd occupied himself by watching infomercials on mute. He'd just gotten to the portion where the host was demonstrating how the super vacuum cleaned pasta sauce from carpet when he heard footsteps approaching. He'd turned off the TV and pretended to be asleep already.

On night two, a documentary about climate change held his interest before Gwen got home, and a Lifetime movie the following night. Today, the fourth day, he was back watching infomercials. He'd been seriously considering calling the number on the screen for the four-in-one pan when Gwen's keys jingled in the door.

Unlike the other nights, where she took care to remain as quiet as possible, Gwen came in and kicked off her shoes and dropped her bags on the tile floor with a thud. She mumbled to herself as she entered the kitchen and flicked on the lights.

In the reflection of the TV, he watched her pour herself a glass of wine and chug it. Evidently, it had been a bad evening.

The sound of glass shattering broke the silence in the apartment, and it was followed by a string of expletives from Gwen.

Anthony was up and out of bed within seconds,

lumbering on legs that hadn't been prepared to move. "You okay?"

"Yeah, I just—" She gestured to the shards of glass that littered the floor like confetti.

"But don't come close. You'll cut your foot open."

He reached for the broomstick tucked away in a very narrow closet next to the fridge and pushed the more visible pieces of glass into a pile before handing Gwen the tool for her to do the same.

It took a few minutes to get the floor swept, and after, Anthony said, "If you want, you can get a piece of bread and dab the floor with it to pick up the tiny pieces we missed."

"That's genius."

They both dropped to their knees with a slice of bread each and spent some time making sure the tile was clear before taking a seat right on the floor.

"I'm sorry I woke you," she said, softly like he might still be asleep.

But he was wide awake, and it partly had to do with the dark green knit dress she wore that rode high on her legs, exposing lush thighs encased in gauzy tights.

"It's fine," he said. "Nothing like a late-night adrenaline pump."

His light comment was met with a lackluster smile, and he zeroed in on how tired she looked.

"You good?" he asked.

She nodded, her large earrings swinging along before she shook her head. "Actually, no."

Something gripped his chest at her words. "Umm. Do you want to talk about it?"

He was as comforting as a cactus, but if he could help, he would.

"It's late," she said.

It was. It was close to eleven p.m.

"Ok—"

"It's just"—Gwen crossed her legs at her ankles and settled against the cabinets—"I had a spectacularly bad date tonight."

He forced himself to maintain a neutral expression. She wanted to talk. About a date. A bad date. A bad date she'd just had.

"W-what happened?"

She massaged her temples. "So Charlie and I go to this board game cafe, and we're having fun, right? We order this fancy coffee, and we're laughing because he keeps forgetting the rules of the game. We're vibing, and I can totally see why we're, like, fifty-nine percent compatible."

How would she even possibly know that? He would have asked, but he didn't want to break her momentum with a question.

"Then suddenly he says something to me… something so rude I didn't know what to say after he said it."

Many possibilities ran through Anthony's head. One worse than the next.

"Like, I've had people say some wild things to me on dating apps, but I'm usually ready for those. I anticipate them. And are you really online dating if someone doesn't ask you if you do anal fifteen minutes into a conversation?"

Jesus.

She suddenly laughed. "And what makes things worse is that I wasn't even too much in my head on this date."

Gwen was obviously working through her feelings as she spoke but killing him in the process. He was wound up so tight waiting for her to reveal what the guy had said, he thought he might pop.

"Gwen, what did he say?" he finally asked when she seemed to forget the point of the entire conversation.

She looked him dead in the eyes before leaning forward and saying, "He said I reminded him of his mother."

The word "mother" came out as if laced with venom.

"At first, I'm in shock, but after I recovered, I was like, "*a* mother or *your* mother?" I felt the distinction was important," she said.

Sure.

"Like, are you calling me attractive in a MILF type of way because I can maybe rock with that. But I don't know how to handle the other thing."

He liked her like this. Biting, irreverent.

"Which one was it?" Anthony asked.

"*His* mother," she said, her irritation giving way to light, bubbly laughter. "Fifty-nine percent compatible, my ass."

"What do you mean by fifty-nine percent compatible?" Anthony finally asked.

His question seemed to knock her out of the little loopy state she was in. She sat up straight and studied him for a moment before saying, "I hired a professional matchmaker, and I've been going on dates with people they set me up with."

There was so much there, but he slammed his teeth together against the impulse to ask her more invasive questions.

"I can't believe I told you that," she said, rubbing the bridge of her nose.

"I'll add it to the list of your secrets I won't tell anyone, right under alphabet burping."

This made her laugh.

"I'm guessing you're not seeing this guy again?" he asked after clearing his throat with a cough.

"No, but I still need to fill out the post-date survey."

One of his eyebrows moved upwards. "The matchmakers make you write a review of your dates?"

"It's not a review. It's an assessment of the different components of the date like the activity, the person, feelings—Okay, yeah, it's a review. But its only goal is to improve the matchmaking formula."

She pulled up something on her phone and handed it to him. "It sounds worse than it is."

Anthony studied the screen for a minute before reading the neatly formatted questions aloud. "'How was your date on a scale from one to ten? How was the chemistry? Can you picture another date with this person?'"

"See? Not bad," Gwen said.

He looked up. "You do this for every date?"

"I do."

"Hmm."

She smiled. "That 'hmm' was real heavy."

"Nah, just seems like a lot of work, that's all."

"You're not the first person to say that," she said. "But in the end, it'll be worth it."

The end being her relationship with some perfect guy. Probably someone who owned multiple suits and read books that doubled as doorstops.

Something hot and foreign churned at the base of Anthony's stomach.

"It's late," she said. "I should go to bed and say a prayer that I don't have a wine-induced headache tomorrow."

They rose from the ground together.

"Thanks for listening to my weird post-date rant."

"Any time."

"You don't mean that," she said, her laughter light.

When she left the area, he got back into bed and was alone again with his thoughts.

Days without interacting with Gwen: 0

Chapter Seven

GWEN WOKE up with a start to the spearing noise of her alarm swatting at the cobwebs of sleep. Rolling over, she grabbed her phone to stop the sound, but when she saw the time, she leaped out of bed.

"Shit," she said.

Wine on a weeknight. Served her right. Her head swam as she made her way to the shower and tried to complete her morning routine at top speed.

She'd never been late to work in her life, and she wouldn't start today. As she tried to shove her arms in a sweater and apply deodorant at the same time, she hobbled to the front door, picking up her bags and keys along the way. She'd just resigned herself to a hungry morning when she caught sight of something on the kitchen counter.

A breakfast sandwich from the shop a couple of blocks away, a bottle of Gatorade, pain killers, and a note that read "For that possible headache."

Gwen pressed her fingertips to her lips to contain a grin. The thought of Tony doing all of this for her before leaving for work made her a bit giddy.

Long after she'd taken the pills and eaten the sandwich, she couldn't stop smiling about it. It had lifted her spirits, so much so that when she went to chat with Raven during recess at the school's office, her friend commented on it.

"Girl, you're glowing. That date must've gone particularly well. Did you… " Her friend winked and playfully whistled.

"No," Gwen said. "Far from it, actually."

Gwen went on to tell Raven about Mr. You-Remind-Me-Of-My-Mom.

"Then what's got you in such a chipper mood today?"

She hesitated before leaning into the high front desk and saying, "Tony left me breakfast and painkillers."

Her friend's eyes widened. "He did? Why?"

"I sort of unloaded on him last night about the date. Wine was involved."

"Wow, okay."

"He was very sweet about it."

"You told me he was a grumpy weirdo," her friend said.

"Okay, I don't think I used the word 'weirdo,' but I might've been too quick to judge."

"Now that's a life lesson," Raven said.

Gwen tended to quickly assess people and pinpoint what they were all about before sorting them into boxes. And she'd done that with Tony, but he turned out to be sort of an enigma that kept surprising her. Delighting her.

"Are you going to take a break?" her friend asked.

"From dating? No, I already have my next four lined up."

The great thing about this process is Gwen didn't have to dwell on the dates that went badly.

"God, with all the effort you're putting in, the guy you end up picking better be an Adonis."

Raven's words rattled around Gwen's head a couple of days later while on a date with a food scientist named Xavier.

They'd decided to attend a pottery class together at a ceramics store. The space had a chill atmosphere, and it was filled with tons of plants and beautiful vases of various sizes and colors. They'd eaten at the attached vegan cafe before the class began, and Gwen could see an overpriced wellness workshop being held there.

She was wrist-deep in uncooperative clay when she leaned over to her date and whispered, "I don't think I'm enough of an Erykah Badu for this."

"What does that mean?" Xavier asked, his voice flat.

"You know, she's all incense and headwraps and…"

Xavier's eyes narrowed behind his glasses as she continued to speak.

Gwen sighed. "It's a joke."

They were a 71% match, but the evening had yet to reveal evidence of that. He seemed unimpressed with her, like he was doing her a favor by even being out with her. If it weren't for the promise she made to herself to put her all into the process, she'd have already left.

Minutes later, she turned to him and said, "I read on your profile you liked—"

"Shh," Xavier said with enough force to send spittle flying from his mouth, his eyes glued to their pottery instructor.

This was the first time she'd been hushed by a man she was dating, and she looked around to see if she'd been dropped onto Mars. It took everything in her not to side-kick his clay off his pottery wheel. She instead poured all her focus into crafting a small vase, and at the end of the date, she had a finished product and a man she would not see again.

When she got home, she slowly unlocked and opened her front door, trying not to wake Tony as she had a few nights ago. But when she stepped inside, she found him sitting on his bed with a book on his lap and the TV playing on very low volume.

She paused at the door for a second and quickly swiped her mouth with her hand to make sure there were no crumbs from the vegan danish she'd eaten on the ride home.

"I didn't expect you to be awake," she said, dropping her bags and removing her boots.

"Couldn't sleep. I'm just reading to tire myself out," he said as he turned to look at her.

She felt the oddest flutter in her stomach when his dark gaze landed on her, but she ignored it to say, "I spent my evening at a pottery class on a date."

She handed him her creation and watched as he turned it over in his hands.

"An ashtray?" he asked.

"It's supposed to be a decorative vase, thank you very much," she said, coming to sit on the armchair in the living room.

"Ah, yes. Now that you say it," he said, but from the overly serious way he nodded and regarded the "vase," she knew he was teasing her.

She reached over across his bed and snatched her art piece. "Screw you."

There was a soft, low chuckle that passed his lips that Gwen might've thought she'd imagined if it weren't for the subtle lift of his mouth.

"So the date was a success?" he asked.

"I wouldn't say that," she said, pausing for a moment before asking, "Like, when I say I'm not enough of an Erykah Badu, what does that mean to you?"

"You're not, I don't know, the spiritual, hippie-dippie type?"

"Okay! Thank you! My date tonight acted like that didn't make any sense, but he didn't say I remind him of one of his family members, so it's an improvement."

"Well, cheers to that," he said.

In the moment of silence that followed, Gwen realized she'd done it again. She was chatting with him like they were just a couple of girlfriends on some rooftop bar during happy hour.

"Sorry. I keep telling you all about my dating life. I should ask you questions."

"About my dating life?" he asked as one of his eyebrows lifted.

"No," she replied with a light snort—but now that he mentioned it, she wondered what kind of woman Anthony Woods went for.

He was an athlete. A former pro one. She was sure he was doing well for himself, but she could only think of one actual girlfriend he'd had, and that was because she'd tried to sell Gwen some godawful-looking leggings when they first met.

"I was thinking about more like, is this what you'd be doing on a regular evening at home? Watching infomercials and reading under bad lightning?"

"Yeah, but probably shirtless."

Now, why had he said that?

She forced herself not to let her eyes fall lower than his impossibly broad shoulders. If anyone else had made that comment, she'd assume they were flirting, but Tony had delivered the sentence so matter-of-factly that she wasn't sure.

"No, I get it," she responded. "I'd probably be pants-less most of the time if you weren't around."

Now, why had *she* said that?

She laughed a little to diffuse her remark and make it sound less flirtatious, but it died abruptly as Tony's gaze lowered and followed the length of her legs. Several feet separated them, but one would think he'd run his hands over her bare skin the way she suddenly grew hot.

Her body's response was so unexpected that she shot up to her feet like she was guilty of something and hastily said, "Look at the time. I better go."

They quickly said good night, and instead of getting ready for bed, Gwen forced herself to complete the post-date survey. And when she'd done that, she scheduled her next date.

————

A crush was easy to handle if said crush was only a collection of vague details and projections. But Anthony had gone from completely avoiding Gwen to knowing the way her brows furrowed when she was indignant and how her nose scrunched up when she found something funny. Not to mention the moans she made when she orgasmed.

It left Anthony feeling unsettled.

He decided to check on the progress of his apartment, praying he'd get lucky and find things ahead of schedule. Maybe he could move back in sooner than expected.

But when he arrived at the landlord's office, he found it locked with a simple notice on the door:

No updates at this time. We will email or text you once things have been resolved. Thanks for your patience.

Straightforward and boundlessly annoying.

Still unsettled, Anthony headed to a place that had made him feel grounded since he was a kid. He slowed down as he entered the familiar residential area Enoch and his wife Katherine still lived in. And as customary, when he was in the neighborhood, he peered out the window to look at his childhood home.

Bicycles lay in the driveway haphazardly, perhaps abandoned for a midday snack. The tree that had been a tiny little thing while he was growing up was now imposing, its leaves just starting to turn shades of yellow and orange.

He felt like he should feel more attached to that house, but those four walls were never that meaningful to him.

Continuing down the road, he arrived at his destination and parked. When he got out, the sound of classical music filled the street, and he followed it to the back of the house. He opened the loud rickety gate and knew what scene would meet him.

Old Man Enoch sat on a lawn chair in front of his giant pumpkin, talking to it while Chopin played on a radio beside him.

"A few more weeks. All you have to do is grow a little more for a few more weeks," Enoch said before turning around and asking Anthony, "How does my girl look?"

Anthony studied the bright orange vegetable with hints of green and yellow that encompassed almost the entire side of the house.

"Large."

"Damn straight," Enoch said. "This one's going to place. I can feel it. And not even Cheating Jeremy can do anything about it."

Anthony retrieved a second lawn chair from the nearby shed and planted it beside the old man's.

"Wasn't expecting you today," Enoch said, looking sideways at him.

"I was in the neighborhood, thought I'd drop by," Anthony replied. Many things had changed in his life, but running to this house for respite had pretty much stayed the same.

"Your apartment fixed yet?"

"Not yet."

"You here for the spare bedroom, then?"

"I came to hang out with you, old man. That's not enough?"

Enoch smiled and went back to whispering to his pumpkin.

"You been spying recently?" Anthony asked sometime later when he noticed tiny scratches marring the older man's hands.

He could picture Enoch ducking behind bushes and rolling out of the way to avoid detection.

"It's from putting up that fence. I needed to stop the wind from getting at the leaves." Enoch turned to the pumpkin and, in a baby voice, said, "Because you need pretty leaves for your debut, don't you?"

"Sweetheart!" Katherine called out as she slid the porch door open. "If I were to kill you, how do you think I'd do it?"

"Well, I'd hope you'd remember the good times and reconsider," the old man said without turning away from the pumpkin.

"Yes, of course, but I'm watching *Dateline*, and this woman—Oh, Anthony," Ms. Katherine said once she spotted him.

The older woman descended from the short porch, and Anthony stood up to meet her halfway.

She cupped his face between her hands, "Have to make sure you're actually here. You haven't visited in a while."

"Sorry, ma'am," he said, his words distorted from the way she squeezed his cheeks. "Been busy."

"Enoch tells me you don't have a home, and you've been living with a stranger," she said flippantly as she released him.

"I still have my apartment. It's just unlivable at the movement. And not a stranger. Duncan's sister, Gwen."

"That's a nice name. Gwen," Ms. Katherine said, pondering for a moment. "Short for Gwyneth."

"Or Guinevere," her husband offered.

She pointed and excitedly said, "Also, Gwenda."

"Gwendoline—"

"I think she just goes by Gwen," Anthony said, cutting them off before they could get carried away.

"So what does she have that we don't have, huh?" Ms. Katherine asked, crossing her arms. "A soft-serve ice cream machine is the only excuse. You know we have a spare bedroom."

"Two!" Enoch added.

"It's closer to Spotlight," Anthony said. If he was being honest, the travel difference was negligible, but the fact was those spare rooms were packed to the brim with all sorts of props and Enoch's half-finished projects. It would've probably taken him the duration of his stay to make it livable.

"Well, if anything changes, you know you're always welcome," Ms. Katherine said.

It never ceased to amaze Anthony how willing the couple were to help him, but they'd been looking out for him for almost his entire life. Even so, he never wanted to intrude, to assume, to take their presence in his life for granted. They had actual children and grandchildren who could have such audacity.

Anthony's own mom and dad were serious, cold people who'd had an old-school parenting style. His childhood was littered with moments where he desperately wanted some sort of connection with his parents and subtly or not so subtly being denied that.

He remembered one particular incident where for a Valentine's Day project at school, he'd been required to cut out these paper hearts and draw the things he loved on them.

Ten-year-old Anthony had included basketball, his bike, his mom and dad, and Beyblade.

When he'd presented the heart meant for his father to him, his dad had been unimpressed. Anthony still could picture his unmoved expression.

Looking back, it was no wonder he'd gravitated towards Old Man Enoch and Ms. Katherine. They had a warmth that emanated from them. Plus, he'd liked hanging out at their place because Ms. Katherine could cook, and Old Man Enoch would let him watch boxing highlights he never seemed to be able to find on the television at home.

"Okay," Ms. Katherine said, pulling him out of his thoughts as she fastened a tight grip on his forearm and started walking them toward the house. "I got some banana bread with your name on it."

———

If anyone dared question Gwen's commitment to finding The One, she'd simply point to the forty minutes she spent battling traffic to meet her matchmaker for their scheduled check-in.

Upon entering the swanky downtown hotel bar, Gwen spotted Mary sitting in the far corner of the dining room typing furiously away on her phone. Gwen dodged low furniture and waitstaff with stacks of dishes to get to her.

"You look great," Mary practically shouted as she jumped up from the plush chair to hug Gwen.

The waiter showed up to take their drink orders once they were seated, and Gwen scanned the expensive menu and said, "I'll have water, thank you."

"I'm picking up the tab today," Mary said in a low voice.

But twenty bucks for a cocktail seemed absurd regardless of who was paying.

"No, water's fine, thank you," Gwen said.

"Sooo, how has your experience with us been so far?" Mary asked after the waiter left. She leaned heavily onto her fists, eyes wide and attentive.

"It's been good," Gwen said, reminding herself not to be evasive. It was literally Mary's job to know these things. "A little overwhelming at times, but I'm feeling confident."

"Anyone you like?" Mary asked.

"Several of them are great guys," Gwen said vaguely, unwilling to hail any one of them as her favorite.

These sorts of decisions couldn't be rushed. She didn't want to prematurely pick someone and find out something that would disqualify him down the line. And with all these resources on her side, wasn't it worth wading through as many options as she could anyway?

"And I'm seeing Nelson again this Saturday," Gwen said. It was supposed to be a date to make up for the one she'd accidentally invited Tony to.

Mary nodded slowly. "We're impressed with how totally and completely committed you are to this process."

Something about Mary's tone had Gwen straightening in her seat. "Is there a problem?"

"No! Not a problem," Mary said. "You're so amazing, but we do have a teeny tiny concern."

"Okay."

"You seem to be a generally ambitious person, which is such a good thing. We need more people like you in society," Mary said, words seemingly falling out of her mouth faster than she could take a breath.

Gwen couldn't even anticipate the critique, but she braced herself.

Mary reached across the table to grasp Gwen's hands. "But you're doing what we call overbooking."

"What?" Gwen asked.

The matchmaker pulled out a tablet from her bag she'd perched on the table. "You've gone on a date with almost every candidate we've matched you with."

"I wanted to seize all opportunities to make a connection," Gwen said, taking in the colorful graph that only made some sense.

"I understand, but in the process, you're not giving yourself any breathing room. For instance, I can bet you can't name the activities you did on your last three dates."

Gwen opened her mouth then shut it. Things *had* begun to run together. Dinners, picnics on cold benches, axe throwing, a comedy show, ice skating, more dinners. But it was a method that assured her that she wasn't accidentally overlooking anyone. And for the money she'd put into this endeavor, she was at least going to say she'd tried her best.

"I know it seems like a lot, but I feel good about my approach," Gwen said.

"Okay, fair," Mary said. "But another downside to your approach is that you're risking running out of candidates."

"I'm sorry, what?"

"With every date you go on, we take your feedback and refine your choices. It narrows the pool."

For some illogical reason, Gwen had believed that there was an endless trove of eligible bachelors waiting for her to just pick them.

"All right," Gwen said, placing her hands neatly on the table. "What should I do?"

It was clear she needed to be open to advice from an expert before she unintentionally sabotaged her efforts.

"Slow down a little. With very driven clients like yourself, we recommend you only go on one date per week. Skip a week even. It'll give you a chance to consider each candidate and smell the roses along the way."

Gwen nodded. Okay, she needed to chill and stop trying to be so efficient and rigid. She could do that.

When the waiter came to drop off drinks, Gwen decided to put the new attitude into action immediately and said, "Actually, I think I will order a cocktail, after all."

Chapter Eight

THE PROCESS of getting ready for dates had evolved for Gwen throughout her life. When she was a teen and in her early twenties, you could guarantee there'd be several women's magazines open to the dating section strewn on her bed as she got dressed. There'd also be a mini break-down and a friend who did makeup telling her to stop blinking as she applied liner on her. Nowadays, Gwen had her go-to outfits, a makeup routine she could do in the back of an Uber, and a self-imposed curfew.

But in an attempt to savor the matchmaking experience like Mary had insisted she do, Gwen made getting ready for her second date with Nelson an entire event. She put on a nostalgic playlist, spent more time than usual on her makeup, and even took a selfie when she was all done.

By the time she left her apartment, she was excited and ready to have fun and not think about scores or compatibility. However, all the enthusiasm evaporated when, while in the elevator, she received a call from her date.

"I hate myself for what I'm about to say, but I can't make it tonight. Work emergency," Nelson said.

Gwen slumped on the back of the elevator wall. "That's okay. We can set something up for another time."

"Yeah. And if you want, I can transfer the tickets for the tour, and you can still go with a friend or something. Or you can try to sell them if you want."

Though she hated the thought of the tickets going to waste, both options seemed like a lot of work to execute. And she was already mentally sifting through the unread books she could start tonight.

The elevator opened on the ground level just as she ended the call, and Tony stood on the other side of the threshold eating an apple slice from a zip lock bag he held.

She hadn't seen him all week, and she was a little surprised at the thrill that ran up her spine at the sight of him. He stepped to the side to allow her to exit, and she said, "Nope, I'm going back up."

He lifted a brow.

"Last-minute date cancellation," she explained as he entered the elevator.

"Sorry about that," he said softly, offering her an apple slice.

She smiled and took the piece of fruit. "Is this my consolation prize?"

"If it consoles you, sure," he said, a whisper of a smile lifting the corners of his mouth.

She took a bite and said, "Feel better already."

Once in her apartment, a thought struck her as they removed their shoes.

"Hey, do you want to go on my canceled date with me?"

Tony, who'd dropped his bags in his makeshift bedroom, looked up and didn't say anything at first.

"I have two tickets for a tour of some historical site in the city," she said.

He continued to stare at her, his jaw working.

"A theater, I think," she added. "I thought I would ask before letting them go to waste."

His silence made her question herself. The last thing he probably wanted to do was hang out with his best friend's sister on a Saturday evening.

"You can say no," she said, forcing herself to laugh. "I'm not going to kick you out of the apartment if—"

"Let me change," he said, pulling items from his suitcase and disappearing into the bathroom.

It was so abrupt that it took Gwen several seconds to realize he'd agreed to go.

"Dress code is casual!" she shouted as she headed to the kitchen.

She opened the fridge, pulled out the hummus container, and found a nearly finished bag of tortilla chips.

Tony returned a few minutes later and asked, "This good?"

She looked up from her snack, and her mouth went dry. "Yeah, it's perfect."

It was the first time she'd seen him out of the dark workout clothes he typically wore. Or at least the first time she was taking notice. He wore a thick cream-colored pullover hoodie with a gold chain tucked underneath and a pair of dark joggers. It was a simple and wholly unremarkable outfit, but he wore it incredibly well.

His shoulders seemed to stretch forever in either direction, and her fingers itched to run across the hard planes of his chest and arms.

"We should get going," Gwen said, yanking herself out of the weird place her thoughts were leading her to.

They left her apartment, and while walking down the hallway, she expected him to change his mind, but he didn't. When they rode the elevator to the ground floor, she was certain he'd make an excuse and bow out, but he remained silent.

Once they were seated in her car, she said, "You still have time to back out, you know."

He answered by fastening his seatbelt.

Generic radio music replaced any conversation they might've had as Gwen drove. She kept her eyes fixed on the road ahead, trying not to read too much into the butterflies swarming around her stomach.

This could be fun.

———

This was going to be torture.

Anthony should've said no when Gwen asked him to go on another man's date, and he had a tough time explaining to himself why he hadn't.

But now that he'd committed to it, all he had to do was get through a dull tour and avoid looking at her for too long.

At the theater entrance, a distracted man on his phone scanned their e-tickets and granted them access into the poorly insulated building. They found a dozen other people waiting for the tour to begin.

Everyone seemed to be loudly cooing and commenting on the foyer like actors paid to get attendees hyped. But to be fair, the theater was beautiful. Anthony studied the delicate but imposing chandelier attached to the high ceiling. The teardrop crystals sparkled and twirled, reminding him of the fancy glassware Ms. Katherine kept in a cabinet in her dining room.

The baroque-like patterned carpets were noticeably worn, and the columns with elegant moldings had seen better days, but there was a charm and a sense of history etched there.

Halfway through his perusal, he felt Gwen's gaze on him. When he turned to look at her, his damned body betrayed him with a stomach flip. She'd done something to her eyes today with makeup. It made them look even bigger than usual.

"Taking you back to your theater kid days, huh?" she said.

"Yes, this feat of architectural design reminds me of my underfunded high school drama program."

Gwen chuckled as the lights in the foyer dimmed. Everyone quieted in time to witness a man with a thin mustache and top hat appear. Like some character in a Fosse musical, the man flicked his wrists and rolled his shoulders as he moved into full view.

"Welcome, welcome, to the Countess Theater! My name is Dion, and I'll be your guide on this evening's ghost tour."

The group applauded while Anthony's blood turned cold.

Ghost?

His eyes darted from corner to corner. What had he gotten himself into?

"You okay?" Gwen whispered as Dion continued his introduction.

Anthony halted his frantic scanning and cleared his throat. "Yeah, I'm fine. Not a fan of supernatural shit, that's all."

He'd been twelve when he'd watched *The Exorcist* at a friend's house. He'd seen the majority of the movie through his fingers, but it still managed to traumatize him. Since then, he'd avoided haunted houses, most horror movies, and acknowledging the existence of Ouija boards.

"You wanna leave?" Gwen asked softly. "It's no problem."

She had to be using her teacher's voice. It was sincere and reassuring. And as easy it would have been to get the hell out of there while he still could, there was some pride to contend with. He'd faced fighters in the ring who, if given the chance, would've worn his intestines as jewelry. Surely, he could handle some intangible beings floating around.

"Nah, I'm good," he said.

Besides, it was an educational tour. How bad could it be?

"This theater is the most haunted place in the city," Dion proclaimed proudly.

Fuck me.

"On this tour, you'll discover how this theater, once known for debuting promising actors and playwrights, became a site of such major paranormal activity. So much so, I now get a discount at a froyo shop and sixteen dollars an hour to tell you about it."

An excited murmur swept the room, and a man wearing a puffy jacket fist-pumped the air.

"This is an EMF meter," Dion said, holding up a small remote-looking device. "All of you will get one, and it will help us locate supernatural entities in the theater."

The man who'd scanned their tickets at the front casually walked around and handed tour participants a meter.

"All you have to do to use it is point and press the big button in the middle. The more beeping and flashing lights, the more intense the presence. I'll let you know the appropriate places to use them."

Goose bumps rose on Anthony's body, but he straightened his back and crossed his arms against the impulse to walk right out.

"Shall we begin?" Dion asked once everyone had a meter.

They left the large foyer to walk through a hallway with yellow wallpaper. The light scones cast weird oblong shadows, but Anthony refused to study them too closely.

"Built at the turn of the twentieth century, the Countess Theater was Franklin A. Reeves's first passion in life," Dion said, taking deliberate dance-like steps. "His second passion was women, because of course it was. What is an esteemed, famous man without the wife he regularly cheats on?"

A light laughter filtered through the group.

"His dream was to bring the grandness of the theater-going experience he witnessed growing up in London to North America," Dion said.

Evidence of that vision was still legible, and Anthony could easily picture theatergoers tittering behind jeweled-embellished hands before a show.

"Coming up on your left is a portrait of Mr. Reeves himself painted by the artist, Daniel Grove," Dion said as everyone huddled together to study the picture of the man who looked unremarkable but nevertheless dignified.

"It took about ten months to build the theater from start to finish, and a few years ago, we found photographs that documented the progress," Dion said, gesturing to the other side of the hallway where a series of eight framed images hung.

Like a flamboyance of flamingos, the tour group raced over to take a look.

"How did this Reeves guy fund this?" asked a middle-aged man who'd been furiously jotting down notes since the start of the tour.

"He'd like you to believe he bootstrapped it, but he got

a significant loan from his grandfather," the tour guide replied.

"This is so cool," Gwen whispered, studying the grainy photographs.

Anthony nodded, but if he were honest, he found it as cool as the knowledge that tomatoes were actually a fruit. So, not very cool.

Gwen's interest was more alluring. He envied the pictures for how they held her attention. She furrowed her brows and pursed her full lips as she took her time with each photograph.

What would it be like to be regarded so intensely by her?

Gwen turned to look at him suddenly, and for a horrifying beat, he feared he'd said his thoughts out loud.

"How you doing?" she asked.

It took him a second to realize she was asking about how he was coping with the haunted environment.

"I'm good," he said, but Gwen didn't look convinced, so he added, "But I promise if I need to faint, I'll give you a heads-up so you have time to catch me."

The smile and the subsequent snort-laugh she let out made whatever spookiness they'd encounter worth it.

Dion called for the group's attention with a whistle and a wave of his hand before guiding them to a set of heavy-looking double doors.

"During a season, 120,000 people crossed this entry to watch magic happen on stage," Dion said as the doors opened seemingly on their own. What was revealed was a spacious, dimly lit auditorium with stiff red seats.

They entered and walked down the drafty aisles toward the awkwardly big stage that Dion said had been reconstructed in the early aughts. New owners had had the misguided idea to revive the haunted theater for large-scale musical productions.

"There are 1,716 seats in here, and you'd have been hard-pressed to find an empty one on a given night," Dion said as he hopped up on the stage.

A young woman who wore an all-black outfit and the thickest platform boots Anthony had ever seen raised her hand and asked, "How do you know this is the most haunted place in the city?"

"The Ghost Research Society. They estimate twenty-nine ghosts reside within these walls, but also, can't you just feel it?"

Wind whistled through the auditorium at that moment, and Anthony's heartbeat faltered at the insinuation.

"Where do the ghosts come from?" someone else asked. "Who were they?"

"It's hard to say who haunted the theater back in the day, but there's evidence that suggests at least some of the ghosts today are scorned performers," Dion said. "If you're lucky, you can catch the sound of dance shoes that resembles a tap routine featured in a play that debuted here."

They all fell quiet and waited for the tap-dancing ghost to appear. In return, a single bang reverberated around the room like a gunshot and made everyone jump.

"Sorry," the woman with the platform boots said bashfully, picking up the umbrella she'd dropped.

"Pull out your EMF meters. We'll spend some time here," Dion said. "See what you can find."

Everyone scattered, eagerly pointing their meters out in front of them like antennas. He and Gwen walked up and down aisles, waving their devices around too, except Anthony deliberately avoided pressing the button that made the meter work.

"I think mine's broken," Gwen said to him when they came to the end of their fourth row with nothing to show for it.

"Mine too," he said, making a whole show of hitting the meter a couple times against the palm of his hand.

"Maybe it's our location," she said. "Do you wanna check out the stage?"

"Sure."

When they made it to the large raised platform, they joined the handful of people they found there and roamed like aimless pigeons.

"Any luck?" Dion shouted, his voice easily traveling through the space.

"I got some action near the back door," a young man using an assistive cane said. "But it only lasted for a few seconds."

"Okay, let's take a couple more minutes, and then we'll head backstage. Maybe we'll have better luck there," Dion said.

Anthony continued with his award-winning performance as ghost hunter until a man with tan skin and a number of piercings on his face approached him and Gwen.

"Hey, sorry to bother you guys," the man said. "I'm Kevin. I'm a part of the Paranormal Interest Group for People of Color. It's a little collective that meets biweekly to talk about all things paranormal."

"Oh, interesting," Gwen said as she accepted the pamphlet the man offered. "Thank you."

He handed Anthony one as well, and he took it but didn't even bother flipping through it.

"Hope to see you at a meeting in the future."

Anthony nodded and waited for the man to turn away

before haphazardly stuffing the brochure into his coat's pocket.

"I'm guessing you'll not be attending," Gwen said, smiling.

"No, I'll not be joining—"

A sudden beeping silenced and garnered everyone's attention. It was a lethargic sound that pulsed through the empty carcass of a room.

"Whose meter is that?" Dion asked.

"It's mine," an older woman said, lifting the blinking device in the air.

"Seems like we've got a visitor, folks!" Dion shouted.

Energized by the tour guide's announcement, chatter erupted as the group started swinging their meters around, looking for similar results.

"I got something," a man said moments later.

"Me, too!"

"Ah! Over here!" another shouted.

"Brilliant!" Dion declared.

The enthusiasm, however, didn't last for long. As more EMFs went off, it became hard to tell where one sound began and another ended.

"It's so loud!"

"What's going on?" someone cried, panic obvious in their voice.

"Hey, let's all calm down," Dion said over the discordant symphony and growing terror. "There's nothing to worry—"

The lights above and around them flickered like spitting flames, and Gwen and Anthony's eyes met. Her shoulders were tense and her eyes wide, and there was nothing more he wanted to do than sweep her up and get them out of there.

"We should leave," he shouted.

Gwen nodded, and he held out his hand for her to take, but without warning, the room went dark. An ear-splitting scream tore through the room, and frenzy ensued.

"Gwen?" Anthony called into the darkness, his voice one of many.

He pulled out his phone for light and swept the beam across the stage.

"Gwen?" he shouted again, blood rushing to his head when he didn't see her.

She couldn't have just disappeared; she'd been right next to him.

God, had she fallen off the stage and was now lying there concussed?

With his heartbeat damn near outside of his chest, Anthony took two strides forward but was stopped in his tracks when the front of his shoe hit something solid. But before he had a chance to make sense of it and lose his shit accordingly, his body began to sink into the floor.

———

A day ago, if Gwen had been asked if she believed in ghosts, she would have said, "Sure," without any real conviction.

But as she felt her body defy the rules of physics and levitate, she was certain a supernatural being was to blame. With her eyes squeezed shut, she started a prayer she remembered from church when she attended with her grandmother as a child.

However, when all went still and quiet, she opened one eye then the other and easily oriented herself. Dusty beams and pulleys, a downdraft that tickled her exposed skin, and muted thumping from above told her she was underneath the stage.

The small space was dimly lit by LED lights running along the edge of the walls, no doubt an addition during the recent reconstruction Dion had mentioned. She searched for a door and cell service but fell short on both accounts. As she started contemplating shouting for help, the ceiling opened up like a sunroof. A moment later, an elevator-type platform descended, carrying an ashen Tony.

"What the fuck," Tony said, looking around as the hole he'd just come through was immediately replaced with a door.

"Welcome," Gwen said.

"What the fuck?" he repeated, his voice loud and resonant in the tiny space.

"I'm thinking we hit a trap door or something," she said.

He hopped off the raised surface and started investigating every corner as she had.

"There's nothing," she said. "We'll have to wait for help."

"I can't believe this," he said, shaking his head.

"I think we're in a better position than…" She nodded toward the ceiling, where they could hear muffled footsteps and screams.

"Who brings someone on a date like this?" he asked.

It was the first time Gwen had thought of Nelson all evening.

"I don't think it was a bad choice," Gwen said.

"This"—he waved his hands wildly—"is not bad?"

"It's unique. Personally, I'd rate it a seven."

"Seven? Seven? Maybe out of a bazillion," Tony said indignantly.

Gwen pressed her lips tightly together to hide her smile. This was the most animated she'd ever seen him. He always seemed in control of his emotions, reserved, erring on the side of silence. It made his current agitated state fascinating to witness.

"I'll admit it's gone off the rails," she said. "But they say confronting a terrifying situation with someone can help attraction and bonding, so if you think about it, it's a perfect date."

"Who's 'they' exactly?" Tony asked, stepping closer as if he genuinely wanted names so he could take it up with them.

"I don't know. Scientists?" Gwen said.

Tony shook his head before crossing his big arms and saying, "I guess all we can hope for now is that they find us before the rats do."

Gwen froze. "Rats? What do you mean rats?"

"You haven't been hearing the squeaking?" he asked.

"Wait, what? Are you messing with me?"

"No."

"Oh, God," Gwen said, surveying the dark ground around her.

"You mean to tell me ghosts are no big deal, but rodents are where you draw the line?"

"First off, they're real, and they move fast. *And* bite."

"Sure, but you can stomp them with the bottom of your boot," he said.

"What about me screams, 'willing to kill a rat?'" she asked, her voice sounding shriller than she intended.

Tony shrugged. "From personal experience, I know you throw a mean punch, so."

"I can't believe you're bringing that up right—"

Gwen grew still, and the hair on her neck stood up as she registered the unmistakable pressure of something scampering across her boot. To her shame, she screeched. And when she took a step backward, her legs hit a beam.

The world tilted, and she accepted her fate: She'd be in

a heap on the crummy floor any second now, confronting the Lord's worst creatures. But a set of strong hands encircled her arms and brought her upright before any of that could happen.

"Tell me, is this still a seven to you?" Tony asked, his voice low.

Over her still pounding heart, Gwen notched her chin upward and said, "Six point five."

Anthony's lips curved into a small smile, and she realized then that he was still holding her. They'd never been this close to each other. She could smell his aftershave, a subtly sweet, woodsy scent that reminded her of toasted cinnamon sticks.

Her eyes followed the solid length of his neck to his wide lips and eventually landed on his dark eyes where the lines that made up his perpetually stern expression had softened.

God, he was handsome.

Why had that even been a debate before? Gwen couldn't unsee it now.

And on a compulsion she'd overthink later, she pushed herself up on her toes and pressed her lips to his.

The kiss, chaste and brief, left Gwen breathless, and she pulled back as if singed by fire. Their eyes met, and the heat she found in his gaze sent a shiver across her skin. She would have remained standing there, unmoving and transfixed, if, in the next instance, Tony hadn't cupped her face in his hands and kissed her.

His soft, full lips melded with hers, eliciting a sound from her throat. She expected him to be rough, but this big man moved with precision as if trying to wring every ounce of pleasure from the simplest of touch.

She dragged her hands up his broad chest, wishing more than anything he hadn't been wearing a coat. When their lips parted and tongues met, warmth unfurled at the base of her stomach, ending in a flutter somewhere lower.

One of his hands migrated to the back of her neck while his thumb caressed her jaw. There was an intensity he was withholding, simmering beneath his skin. What would it be like to have all that energy focused on her? Perhaps he'd roughly grab her ass, or maybe he'd tighten his grip around her neck. The thought of the possibilities had her deepening their kiss.

But those heightening feelings that had her losing herself in their rhythm and pressing more firmly into his embrace came to a screeching halt when the basement they stood in was suddenly flooded with light.

Gwen gasped as if she was breaking the surface of the water for the first full breath of air.

"Hello?" someone called out from above.

She and Tony backed away from each other, looked up, and found Dion peering down at them from a square hole in the stage.

"We're coming," their tour guide shouted. "Hang tight."

Most of the light disappeared as the door shut, and the reality of what they'd done settled in. Neither of them said a word or looked at each other, but Gwen wanted to know what he was thinking. Was heat pulsing through his body like it was for her?

She thought maybe she could throw out a joke or brush the whole thing off with a comment, but the tension between them held steady until Dion and another staff member arrived to set them free.

They returned to the upper level, where the rest of the group were slumped against different surfaces, stunned and breathing heavy as if at the end of a foot race. Dion profusely apologized to them all and explained that the erratic EMF meters were set off by a delivery truck parked outside full of electronics.

He offered everyone a tote bag with the tour company's logo, but most, including Gwen and Tony, hightailed it out of the building without one.

The drive back to Gwen's apartment was filled with nothing but the sound of her car's engine. When they got inside her apartment, she removed her boots and coat and only then glanced over at Tony.

He was already looking at her but with an unreadable expression. Meanwhile, she feared that everything she was feeling was plainly scribed on her face. She needed to get out of there.

"Okay, well, good night," she said, not waiting for him to respond before she fled to her bedroom.

Chapter Nine

"WHAT DO YOU THINK OF THIS?" Gwen's mom asked, holding up a collection of infant bodysuits and tops.

They were in a small boutique, shopping for Gwen's cousin's baby shower in a few weeks. The store was a sea of pastels as far as the eye could see, and the same three nursery rhymes had been playing from speakers above since they'd entered.

Gwen frowned looking at the garment her mom held up. "Honestly, I don't like it."

"What? It's chic," her mom said, taking another look at the tiny outfits.

"Is it? It looks like clothing for infants living in the post-apocalypse," Gwen said, feeling the distressed fabric.

"The earth *is* on fire, so it's appropriate," her mom said as she placed the clothes in the small shopping basket in the crook of her arm.

"Whatever you say."

"How are you doing, anyway?" her mom asked as they continued their perusal of the store.

"What?" Gwen asked too sharply. "Why?"

"What do you mean 'Why?' It's not a difficult question, Gwendolyn. I'm asking you how you are."

"Oh," said Gwen as she shook herself internally. "I'm good. Work's good. Dating's going well. Etcetera. Etcetera."

She was still flustered because of the kiss with Tony last night. It felt like everyone could tell that it happened. As if the truth was emblazoned on her chest.

It probably didn't help that the memory of the moment was never far away from her mind. Tony's solid body and his soft, encouraging lips bombarded her thoughts every chance she gave it to wander.

Halfway down an aisle, her mom turned and asked, "Are you on edge because Eric's in town?"

Gwen stopped in her tracks. "How do *you* know that?"

"He posted about it on Instagram."

"Mom, why do you still follow my ex on social media?"

"He didn't stop following me, and I thought it would be rude to unfollow him."

"Jesus. Okay? That's fine, I guess," Gwen said, throwing up her hands in resignation. "But yeah, he's in town for his nephew's birthday, and I dropped off the last of his belongings earlier this week. It was not a big deal. We're friendly. No animosity."

"Oh, that's good… So you saw his hair then?" her mom asked with a frown.

"You mean his Sisqó cosplay? Yes, I did."

Gwen had gasped when her ex-boyfriend opened the front door of his sister's home. His once-dark hair had been poorly dyed platinum blonde. He still had his usual cut, but a dramatic design had been carved out on the side of his head. It was a confusing choice because the man had a stuffy job as a database administrator.

In the back of Gwen's mind, there'd always been this

lingering question of whether she'd given up on her relationship with Eric too easily. But for some reason, seeing him with his jarring new hairdo brought her total peace around her decision. Raven would probably call it cosmic confirmation or something else equally pretentious.

"I think he's dating the hairdresser that did it to him," her mom said conspiratorially. "She's all over his page."

"Okay, enough," Gwen said. "Do you realize we've talked about nothing else but love and men? We should discuss other things."

"Gwen, no one can hear us," the older woman said. "Our feminist cards are safe—"

"Like, have you watched any good shows recently? Any funny stories from work?"

Her mom looked at her for a beat before saying, "Fine. I booked a colonoscopy, and I'm making my way through *The Sopranos*."

"Ooh, fun!" Gwen replied. "Look at us talking about diverse subjects."

Her mom rolled her eyes and continued her trek around the store, and Gwen knew the moratorium on discussing her love life wouldn't last very long.

But hopefully the next time her mom inquired about her dates, she wouldn't be consumed with thoughts about Tony and could talk about some guy named Fred or Bob.

———

"Remember, it's smile, point, point, point, body roll, *then* jump," Milo said.

Anthony looked at their social media manager as the guy, once again, demonstrated the steps for a video he was filming for some social media app or another.

"What am I pointing at?" Anthony asked.

"That doesn't matter right now, just point. I'll write the text later."

Duncan had seemed to get it on the first few tries and was standing off to the side, really enjoying Anthony's struggle.

It was unbelievable. He'd conditioned his body for more than a decade to move how it did, but for the life of him, he couldn't correctly twist and contort for a silly sixty-second video.

He tried one more time, making sure to show his teeth so Milo wouldn't accuse him of frowning again.

Milo studied the footage for a long time before saying, "This is fine. It is perfectly satisfactory. I'm not going to sweat the small stuff."

"Happy to underwhelm," Anthony said, dropping his painful grin.

"Oh, and before I forget," Milo said, pulling out two files from his backpack, "here's the report you guys asked for. I've emailed you copies as well."

Anthony took the document and flipped through it, looking at the numbers that showed that their social media engagement had marginally improved. Traffic to their website had also increased, but the conversion to actual paying customers was negligible.

"These things take time," Milo said, misreading their silence as disappointment.

"Oh, we get it, man," Duncan said. "Thank you for the work you're doing."

There was no reason to freak out yet. All they could do was remain consistent. Milo left after they bid him a good day, and Anthony and Duncan began cleaning up all the equipment they'd pulled out to use as props for the videos.

"Your new caller ID photo," Duncan said, holding up his phone to Anthony's face.

The picture showed Anthony in mid-twirl. He looked stressed and confused.

"It's almost as good as yours," Anthony said, pulling out his phone to show his friend the image he'd captured of him looking equally as goofy.

Once they'd cleared the gym floor, they headed upstairs to prepare for opening.

"Hey, by the way, how's your mystery woman?" Duncan asked, placing fresh towels in the cubbies near the front area.

He'd hoped his friend had forgotten all about that.

"And before you say there isn't any woman," Duncan said, "don't bother. I know you, man."

Anthony was silent before he said, "Okay, what about her?"

It was sort of an admission he could have sworn he'd never make, but he needed to talk.

"How are things going?" Duncan asked as if approaching a skittish animal.

His and Gwen's little ghost tour days ago had changed a lot of things. That kiss had felt like getting kicked into a pool of ice-cold water. Exhilarating and panic-inducing.

"We hung out," Anthony said.

"That's good! Right?"

He didn't know anything anymore. A few short weeks ago, he thought he had a system down to get through living with Gwen without much contact. Now he didn't know if he could make it to the end unscathed. In a loop in his head was the memory of her soft lips, her eager hands, and a body he wished he could explore more.

"It's worse than I thought," Duncan said.

"What're you talking about?" Anthony asked.

"Does she even know you like her, man?" Duncan asked. "With that face of yours, she might not even know you like her as a person, let alone know you're interested in her romantically."

"I don't even know if that's what I want," Anthony said, rubbing his head roughly.

"Of course it's something you want. You're all worked up about it."

"I'm not worked up," Anthony said gruffly.

Duncan raised his hands. "Okay, not worked up. But you're definitely overthinking this. And I get it, but you have to put your cards on the table," his friend said. "Flirt or something."

"Flirt?" Anthony asked. "That's your sage advice?"

"A smile, some eye contact, and engaging conversation will take you far," Duncan said.

He made it sound as simple as a box cake recipe, but Anthony knew it wouldn't result in any masterpiece for him. His friend breathed, and people were charmed.

"I think that's easier for you than for me," Anthony said.

"Okay, okay," Duncan said, dropping what he was doing to come over to where Anthony stood before touching his shoulder and saying, "Hey, Anthony."

He looked at his friend. "What are you doing?"

"Showing you how to flirt. Hey, Anthony."

"I promise you, you don't have to do this."

"That's what friends are for. Now, *hey, Anthony*."

"What am I supposed to do?"

"Be yourself. But flirtatious."

"Okay?" Anthony replied. "Hi, how's it going?"

Duncan shrugged. "Better now that you're here. How're you?"

"Good. Thanks?"

"Okay, I gave you the perfect setup, and you wasted it," Duncan said. "Compliment me or something."

Anthony looked his friend up and down, searching for something to take note of. "Nice… outfit."

"Nice is such a whack, toothless word. Give me something better."

"You look beautiful?"

"Okay, great. Just don't make it sound like a question. You don't want her to think you're lying."

"Okay, I think we're done," Anthony said as he pushed his friend out of his way.

"My God, what are you afraid of?" Duncan asked.

How could Anthony explain in a non-pathetic way that his instinct, the one that served him well in the boxing ring, was to guard himself, keep people at a distance? But Gwen was the type of woman he'd have to pull that down for. She'd demand it. Maybe not directly, but he could see her growing frustrated with his emotional opacity.

His past relationships—if you'd call them that—had been fleeting and fun. Ones that his globe-trotting career had inhibited from growing deeper. And it had worked for him. It still did, even if it was getting harder to remember that.

And besides, Gwen deserved someone who could give all of themselves and didn't need tips on how to flirt.

"Nothing, man. I appreciate the advice," Anthony said. "I'll think about using it."

But he suspected they both knew that was a lie.

Chapter Ten

"I MADE OUT WITH TONY."

Raven looked up at Gwen, mouth agape. Her heavy, dramatic lashes fluttered as she blinked repeatedly.

"I know, I know," Gwen said.

The two friends were at the Fall Harvest Festival. They'd arrived early in the morning for the gingerbread pancakes, and now they strolled through the arts and crafts section on the festival grounds.

"All I asked was if you liked the pink or the yellow, and you just drop that without warning?" Raven said, still holding up two tea towels.

"I've had to get that off my chest for days," Gwen said before pointing to the yellow towel in her friend's hand.

"Wait. Days?" Raven asked, abandoning the towels altogether to focus on Gwen. "Okay, break this down for me. How did this even happen?"

"We got stuck under the stage at a haunted theater," Gwen said as they moved to the next table that sold hand-made jewelry.

"As one does. And?" Raven said.

"And then I went in for a kiss, and it was… incredible."

Since that day, however, Gwen had avoided Tony by adopting a toddler's sleep schedule. If she didn't have an evening date, she'd quickly eat her dinner and shut herself in her bedroom for the night.

But being a coward, she'd learned, was a humbling activity. She snuck around her own home like some interloper, and for her trouble, had stubbed her toe on the leg of her entry table more times than she'd care to remember.

"Wait. Do you like him?" Raven asked, grabbing Gwen's arm. "Are you done with the matchmaker?"

"No! No, of course not," Gwen said. "I've spent way too much money with Hearts Collide to even think of abandoning them."

"But if you like Tony, then—"

"No, I find him attractive, but we're not compatible in any other way," Gwen said.

That very logical thought didn't stop her from thinking about the kiss in excruciating detail, though. But all she had to do was hold out for a couple more weeks until Tony left, and she'd get her apartment back as well as her headspace.

Her friend stopped them in the middle of the pathway of the market and said, "Okay, I know you don't really believe in my woo-woo stuff, but…"

"What?"

"I'm just saying all of your interactions with Tony seem synchronous. Like the universe is pointing you and him in the same direction."

Gwen sighed and looked to the sky.

"Think about it," Raven insisted. "Him staying at your apartment in the first place. That accidental dinner you guys had. Then the kiss—"

"Okay, love you, Ray, but the stars or moon or what-ever the hell are not going to dictate my life."

Raven gave her the kind of smile you give a puppy trying to climb a set of stairs.

Gwen rolled her eyes. There was no use arguing.

"Okay, let's bench this convo," Gwen said. "We're going to be late for chicken karaoke."

They walked through the busy market area, bypassing loud vendors and overzealous customers to arrive on the other side, where they found a spot to stand amongst a waiting crowd.

"Nice to see they spelled 'karaoke' right this year," Raven said, pointing to the banner strung up above the stage.

"Nothing less for this high-brow affair," Gwen responded.

What to say about chicken karaoke?

Well, Gwen remembered when she'd attended her first one, she had thought it the most ridiculous thing in the world. But over the years, she had grown oddly invested and fond of it. She even had a favorite chicken, Eggbert.

"If I could get everyone's attention," said the announcer, a middle-aged woman wearing a combo of denim and plaid. "It's good to see another great turnout, and I welcome you all to the Tenth Annual Chicken Karaoke."

"Let's go!" someone shouted as the crowd clapped and hooted.

"As a reminder, please refrain from applause till the end of a song. The chickens can get spooked otherwise," the woman said.

Suddenly, a man appeared on stage, carrying a plat-form decked out in tinsel. It was the miniature stage the chickens would stand on during their performances.

"I want you all to give it up for our first clucker, Hen Solo, who will be performing her rendition of a Céline Dion classic," the announcer said as the crowd applauded.

The bodacious hen was plopped on the small stage in front of a microphone while the backing track for the ballad began. The audience fell silent, waiting.

But the first verse came and went, and all Hen Solo did was bob her neck, unbothered by the progressing song or her handler urging her on from the sidelines.

"They look bored," Raven whispered to Gwen, referring to the judges seated at a table near the front.

Indeed. There was no way this chicken was getting a good score.

But just as the song was going into its second chorus, Hen Solo managed to let out a cluck and finish out strong.

The few performers that came afterward had somewhat better showings, but it wasn't until Eggbert's turn that things started looking up. The chicken, simply put, was a star with his shiny brown feathers and bright yellow beak. Before he even made it to the stage, he was clucking.

"Come on, Eggbert!" someone shouted.

Gwen threw a cursory look in the direction of the excited spectator and fellow Eggbert fan and did a double-take when she spotted a familiar figure in the crowd.

Tony.

He stood a few meters to her left. It was not hard to see him with his head towering above everyone else's. This was the last place she'd expect to see him. The man was full of surprises. She couldn't take her eyes off of him. He had his typical stoic expression set, and it was so out of place in the kitschy environment that it was kind of comical. Like maybe he was one of the chicken's bodyguards.

The sound of applause momentarily brought Gwen back to Eggbert's performance, which she'd missed in its entirety. But from the fervor with which the crowd clapped, she could tell he'd done a great job with the Ariana Grande song. When she went in for another look at Tony, her eyes clashed with his dark ones.

Sharp little tingles ran across her entire body as they held eye contact. She smiled, hoping it read as "very totally chill and not at all freaking out."

He responded with a nod.

"Who you looking at?" Raven asked.

"Uh. No one," Gwen said, turning to face the stage once again.

But Raven was craning her neck and making a whole effort to get a glimpse of what had caught Gwen's attention.

"Please, stop," Gwen said through clenched teeth. "It's Tony, okay?"

"What? He's here?" she asked.

"Yeah."

"Did you know he was going to be here?" her friend asked.

"Obviously not."

"Huh," Raven said smugly. "How *synchronous*."

Gwen wrinkled her nose and settled back in to listen to the remaining chickens, all the while forcing herself not to look back over at Tony. She planned to make a quick escape once the showing was through.

But when the time came to leave the contest after a chick named Meryl Cheep took first place, she and Raven were stuck moving at the glacial pace of the general crowd. And it became clear from how they were all funneling out that she and Tony would at least have to cross paths.

"Shit. Shit. Shit," Gwen chanted under her breath moments before coming face to face with the man she'd avoided all week.

"Hey," Tony said.

Simply seeing him had her stomach in a tizzy, but hearing his voice felt like she'd been catapulted to the moon. It seemed deeper. More robust somehow.

"Hello," she replied.

For several moments she was stuck staring at him, flailing for something appropriate to say. But her dilemma of how to fill the silence was solved when an older woman who she'd just noticed said, "Gwen! So nice to finally meet you."

The woman had silver hair and freckles that dusted her light brown face.

"You Gilmore siblings really have great bone structure," the older woman said as she pushed down her glasses to get a better look at Gwen.

"Thank you," Gwen said, delighted by the unexpected compliment.

"Oh, and I'm Katherine," the woman added quickly. "And this is my husband, Enoch."

"How do you do?" the old man with the shiny bald head said as he dipped low to give a bow.

"Nice to meet you both," Gwen said, smiling at the couple who had energy and smiles that could light up the solar system. "You're Tony's…?"

"Self-appointed godparents," Mr. Enoch said.

"And I'm Raven, Gwen's friend. I think it's awesome that we bumped into you guys here of all places. It's almost synchronous."

Gwen gave her friend a look.

"I hope Anthony is being a good houseguest," Ms. Katherine said.

"Yes, completely," Gwen replied, her eyes flicking upward to meet Tony's.

"Good. That's good!" the older woman said.

There was a brief lull in the conversation before Ms. Katherine asked, "What are you gals doing right now?"

"We were just about to head home, right?" Gwen said pointedly.

"Yeah, but we also kind of talked about staying for a little while longer," Raven said as she avoided making eye contact with Gwen.

"Well, Enoch is competing in the Giant Pumpkin Weigh-off if you want to come and root for him with us," Ms. Katherine said.

"Yeah, I need all the support I can get. I'm going up against real stiff competition," the old man said.

"Of course, we'd love to see your giant pumpkin," Raven said.

"Angels!" Enoch declared.

Tony's expression was impenetrable, but Gwen couldn't imagine him being too thrilled about his godparents' invitation.

"It starts in an hour, but we're heading over there now to get good spots," Ms. Katherine said, looping her arm through her husband's.

"Lead the way!" Raven said.

"What are you doing?" Gwen whispered to her friend as they followed behind the older couple and Tony.

"Nothing. I want to watch giant pumpkins get weighed," Raven said.

"Bullshit."

But there was no escaping now, or at least that's what Gwen told herself as she made no effort to excuse herself from this detour.

After a few minutes' walk across the yellow carpet of leaves, they arrived at a horse-drawn hayride that would take them to the pumpkin weigh-in site.

When the attendant helping passengers on board

declared there were only a few more seats left for this trip, Raven shoved her way past Tony to get the last seat on the ride with the older couple. It left Gwen and Tony waiting to catch the next one.

Her friend waved at her as the horse trotted away, and Gwen nearly flipped her off. She snuck a look at Tony, who was looking at everything but her. So she followed suit, studying the bright blue sky and the almost bare trees. But she soon realized that this was the perfect time to clear the air.

"I—"

"There—"

They said at the same time.

"Sorry, go ahead," Tony said.

"Oh, no, I was just going to bring up that thing that happened on the ghost tour," she said, feeling her blood pressure spike and her hands grow too hot for her gloves.

"Okay," he said after clearing his throat.

"It was meaningless. A nothing kiss. And I don't want you to think I'm trying to get with you or anything."

She held her breath as she waited for him to respond.

"We're good," he said.

Those simple words were meant to dissolve the awkwardness between them, but Gwen did not feel the release.

———

Meaningless.

As Anthony sat beside Gwen on the hayride, he turned the word over in his head. He'd been locked in a week-long battle with himself, trying to forget that kiss, but Gwen regarded it with nothing but apathy.

What a humiliating state he was in.

But even the knowledge of unreciprocated lust couldn't curb the electric-like zaps he felt every time the cart jostled and Gwen's thigh rubbed up against his. But salvation came when they finally reached the top of the hill.

Despite the numerous times Anthony had attended this event, he was always thrown by how large the pumpkins looked lined up against the horizon.

"There they are," Gwen said, pointing to the trio that had gone ahead of them. They sat close to the front on some hay bales.

As they neared, Anthony watched Ms. Katherine shove food into her husband's hand and say, "You have to eat something, Enoch. You're going to pass out on that damn forklift."

Enoch had been nervous all morning and had zero appetite as a result, but reluctantly, he took a mini donut and stuffed it in his mouth.

"Happy?" he asked.

"Yes," Ms. Katherine said before acknowledging Gwen and him. "Come on, come on. There's space for everybody."

Again, Anthony found himself squished next to Gwen, and this time it was the scent of her perfume wafting toward him on a breeze that tormented him.

"Okay, wish me luck!" Enoch said as he solicited high-fives from all of them before jogging off to join the other weigh-off participants who all seemed to be dressed for different events. A few looked like regular farmers, but others were outfitted as if going to their office jobs, a sweet sixteen party, and even a night out.

Ms. Katherine and Gwen's friend immediately got caught up in a seemingly humorous conversation, leaving him and Gwen out of it.

Several minutes passed with neither one of them

speaking, and it had him wishing he was the whistling type so at least he wouldn't feel like he was drowning in the dead air.

"You come here every year?" Gwen asked him suddenly.

"Only since the old man's been competing."

"Cool."

The hearty laughter from Ms. Katherine and Raven at that moment seemed to underscore the staleness of the conversation between him and Gwen.

But his endurance was rewarded when the competition officially commenced, and the announcer welcomed everyone and introduced the participants.

Cynthia Teller's pumpkin was up first, and spectators watched with bated breath as she maneuvered her giant gourd onto the scale with the provided forklift.

Nobody wanted to see anyone's pumpkin splatter into bits before it was weighed, so when Cynthia made a successful transfer, people applauded. Her vegetable came in at 1,101 pounds, which Anthony knew was on the lower end.

Peter Singh and Lenessa Reed had respectable weights in the 1,500-pound range, whereas Gavin Palmer's entry came in well under everyone else's. But the symmetry and almost cartoonish orange of Palmer's pumpkin would at least guarantee him the "Most Beautiful" ribbon.

When it was finally Jeremy's turn, a few scattered boos swept the audience, and even from where Anthony sat, he could see Enoch's nostrils flare.

"Am I missing something?" Gwen whispered to him.

"He's a suspected cheater."

Many anticipated Jeremy's weight to blow the previous ones out of the water, and it did just that. Plus, he maintained his lead against the next six contestants.

"Oh, Enoch's next," Ms. Katherine said as she clapped her gloved hands and waved at her husband.

The old man got into the forklift and worked the prongs underneath his pumpkin before slowly inching it toward the scale. At one point, the plump gourd wobbled like it might tip over and fall, and Gwen reached over and grabbed Anthony's forearm briefly. It was a mindless action, but she might as well have had a grip around his lungs.

Once the pumpkin was properly situated on the scale, the numbers started moving, surpassing several contestants' final weights, and for a moment, Anthony thought it actually might be the old man's year. But the number unceremoniously stopped climbing, landing Enoch squarely in the middle of the pack and guaranteeing he wouldn't place.

"Shit," Anthony said.

"It's all right, baby!" Ms. Katherine shouted.

Anthony knew whatever disappointment the old man was feeling would triple if Jeremy won, which it was increasingly looking like it would be the case.

"We'll have to stop at his favorite barbeque joint for dinner. The ribs always cheer him up," Ms. Katherine said to him.

The last competitor, Esmeralda Santos, was a first-time entrant with a misshapen dark green and orange gourd. As she sat her pumpkin on the scale, you could tell the audience's lack of confidence in her because many were already chatting amongst themselves. It seemed inevitable that Jeremy would win for the fourth year in a row.

But the idiom about not counting your chickens before they hatch could be applied to giant pumpkin weigh-offs because Esmeralda's pumpkin not only won the title of heaviest pumpkin, but it did it by a landslide.

That meant that Jeremy, for the first time in three years, would not be number one, and that fact made contestants and audience members alike clap and cheer.

The trophies and ribbons were handed out, and all the while, Enoch, with no prize to claim, had a grin on his face. When he approached his wife, it was with a pep in his step.

"For God's sake, Enoch, try not to look so gleeful," Ms. Katherine said. "Pretend to have some sportsmanship."

"I may have lost the battle, but we won the war, baby! Jeremy has been defeated!" He kissed Ms. Katherine before pointing at Anthony and saying, "What did I tell you?"

Anthony could do nothing but smile.

They all took the same hayride back to the main festival grounds, and Anthony ended up sitting between a stranger and Old Man Enoch, while Gwen sat across from him with her friend. Whatever the two women were talking about had Gwen rolling her eyes one moment and throwing her head back as she laughed the next. She was captivating to watch.

"You're falling for her."

Anthony turned to the stranger who'd spoken to him, a woman with a toque pulled low over her ears.

"What?" he asked, his voice suddenly hoarse.

The older woman smiled at him. "I said, I wish it was fall all year."

"Oh. Yeah, sure," Anthony replied, shaking himself.

When they finally arrived, the five of them hopped off the cart and coincidentally proceeded in the same direction.

"Have you tried the apple cider?" Ms. Katherine asked the two younger women as they neared a kiosk of the homemade drink.

"No, is it good?" Gwen asked.

"Oh, you've got to try it," Enoch said. "It'll change your life."

"Sold," Gwen said as she and Raven pulled out their wallets.

"I got it," Anthony said, stopping them from retrieving their money.

"You sure?" Gwen asked.

"Absolutely," Anthony said before heading toward the station for the drinks.

It was a reprieve he desperately needed.

While he waited in line, he turned to his left to watch and listen to a three-person bluegrass band performing under a large tent. Children and adults were dancing around the stage to the lively song.

When he finally made it to the front of the queue, he ordered and paid for the drinks before stepping off to the side to pocket his change. While trying to figure out a placement that would allow him to carry all four cups without spilling anything, there was a commotion that made him look up.

People were shouting, running, and waving their hands, and it took Anthony several seconds to understand what all the hysteria was about.

A giant pumpkin was rolling down the hill they'd just descended at full speed, crushing kiosks and tables along the way.

Most people swerved and jumped out of the pumpkin's path, but Anthony tracked its eventual destination and saw a couple of kids there, none the wiser to the large vegetable barreling at them.

"Move! Move!" Anthony shouted, dropping the cups as he sprinted towards the children.

He was trying to outrun a gourd with size and

momentum on its side. With movements mostly born out
of instinct, Anthony pushed himself to run faster.

There was a moment when he didn't think he'd make
it; the kids seemed too far away.

But as soon as he was close enough, he lunged and
shoved them out of the way. It was seconds before a solid
weight hit him from the side and threw him to the ground.
He lay there for a moment, not feeling much but the
stringy, orange guts of the now-demolished pumpkin
raining down on him from above.

His last thought before everything went black was "I
better not fucking die from a giant pumpkin."

Chapter Eleven

THE LIGHT WAS what Anthony comprehended first. There was so much of it he struggled to open his eyes fully. For some reason, he immediately decided he must be dead and in hell. Sure, it didn't look like the hell described behind a pulpit, but it wouldn't be the first time humans were wrong about something.

But when he finally opened his eyes, he saw her face.

Gwen.

Okay, definitely heaven. There must've been a glitch in the system, but dammit, he wouldn't mention it if this was what his days would entail.

She was gazing down at him with a soft expression. Her dark skin looked luminescent, her brown eyes bound-lessly deep.

He opened his mouth, and Gwen leaned in closer and touched the side of his face with the back of her hand.

"You're so beautiful," he croaked.

It seemed like the silliest thing to say at the moment, but it was the only thing he wanted to say.

"What was that?" someone, not Gwen, asked.

The voice broke through the muddle around Anthony, and the pain all across his body came into focus as well as the sounds that weren't so distant anymore. The sterile smell of the hospital was the last thing to hit him.

Damn, he was alive.

"I don't know," Gwen said. "Tony, what did you say?"

Anthony attempted to push himself up, but it felt like forces greater than gravity were working against him.

"Relax, son. Relax," Enoch said, appearing from the side to gently guide him back down.

As the memories of what happened came flooding back, Anthony asked, "The kids okay?"

He hadn't seen where they'd landed before he'd passed out.

"They're fine. Scraped knees and a bit of a scare," Ms. Katherine replied.

Anthony nodded as tension released from his shoulders.

When a cell phone in the room rang, Gwen answered it, and Anthony heard his best friend ask, "Is he awake?"

Gwen handed him the phone where Duncan was pressed close to the camera on a video call.

"Damn, man, you scared the shit out of us," his friend said.

"Yeah, I'm fine. I just wanna get out of here," Anthony said, shifting in the scratchy hospital gown.

"We have to wait for the doctor," Ms. Katherine said.

And as if on cue, the doctor arrived with her clipboard and pen tucked behind her ear.

"How are you feeling, Mr. Woods?" the doctor asked.

"Like I got hit by a giant pumpkin," Anthony replied.

He hadn't meant the comment as a joke, but everyone, including the doctor, laughed.

"Well, you're quite a hero," she said.

Before he could protest or feel uncomfortable with the moniker, the doctor jumped into conducting a few cognitive tests. The examination yielded no worrying results, and all he had to contend with was a few bruised ribs and a headache for a day or two. The worst part of his situation was that the doctor recommended he not work for a week.

"The business will manage without you," Duncan said. "Stay home and put your feet up."

The doctor gave him the clear to head home, and he was discharged with some painkillers and a cup of fluorescent green Jell-o.

While standing outside near the front of the hospital, Ms. Katherine said, "We'd offer you the spare bedroom again, but I have a feeling you'd say no." Her eyes flitted to Gwen who stood a few meters away from them, wrapping up the call with her brother.

Anthony opened his mouth to ask her what she meant, but Ms. Katherine silenced him with a kiss on his cheek.

"Feel better, sweet boy," she said.

Next, the old man hugged him and said, "We'll talk soon."

Once he and Gwen arrived at her place, he ate leftover lasagna and took an unintentionally slow shower that improved his mood and sore muscles. Exiting the bathroom, he found Gwen in her kitchen, leaning over the counter as she read a paperback.

"Got nervous there for a second. You were taking so long," she said, placing her book down to look at him.

"Limited range of motion and all," he said, walking over to the couch. He couldn't wait to sink into the mattress and feel the cool sheets. But the moment he applied force to pull the bed out, a sharp twinge ripped through the side of his body.

"Dammit," he said as he let go of the handle.

"What's wrong?" Gwen asked, joining him in the living room.

"Having trouble opening the bed," he said, distressed to find himself out of breath.

"Oh, God. I didn't even think about that, and I can never do it on my own," she said as she took hold of the loop on the pull-out couch and tugged at it for several seconds. It barely budged.

"Let me try again," he said.

"Don't hurt yourself."

Anthony gave all he had into this pull, and in return, his vision blurred for a second.

"I guess I'm sleeping on top of the couch," he said once he could see again.

It was not a very wide or long couch and seeing as he was already in pain, he wasn't looking forward to finding out how exactly his body would rebel in the morning.

"No. You're not sleeping on the couch," Gwen said. "You're way too big, and you literally just got body-slammed by a pumpkin. You'll just have to sleep in my bed for the night."

He shook his head. "I'm not kicking you out of your bed."

"Oh, I meant we would share it. I've passed out on this couch one too many times, and the crick in my neck isn't worth it," she said.

Share a bed with Gwen. He didn't know how to compute the information for several moments.

"I don't snore, and the bed is a queen-size. Lots of room," she said.

"A-as long as you're comfortable with it."

"Great, it's settled then," she said, nodding as if they'd agreed to something trivial like what they'd eat for dinner.

When he entered her room, he zeroed in on her bed. It was big, sure. But not big enough.

"I'm just going to take a shower. You can get in," she said before leaving.

Her room was tidy and minimally decorated. A few books sat on top of her dresser, and she had large fans hung up on her wall. When he slipped into her bed, he was immediately met with the lavender scent permeating her sheets. He didn't know a scent could turn him on, but as he lay there staring at the ceiling, he could admit he was slightly horny.

Gwen eventually returned wearing a matching pajama set with the buttons done all the way to the top and a scarf around her head.

"Thought I'd find you out cold," she said before turning off the lights.

He watched her, silhouetted in the moonlight, move across the room and slip into the spot beside him. The bed was definitely not big enough; he could feel her body heat and smell her clean skin. This was going to be a long night.

"Do you need more pillows or an extra blanket?" she asked.

"I'm good, thanks," he said, still on his back and breathing shallowly.

A minute of silence followed before she spoke again. "Can I ask you a question?"

He turned his head to look at her. His eyes had adjusted to the dark, but still, he could only see minimal details. "Sure."

"I'm curious how this injury compares to when you used to fight."

"Pain-wise, it's not the worst I've felt, but I know my tolerance has gone down since I've gotten older, and I'm not on the pro-boxing grind anymore, so."

"I've never seen you fight," she said.

"There're some videos up on YouTube."

"Wait," she said as she rolled over and grabbed her phone, the light breaking the darkness and illuminating her face. "Do you mind if I watch one?"

"Go ahead," he said, studying her as she typed his name into the search bar, resulting in half a dozen videos popping up.

"Which one do you recommend?" she asked.

He pointed at the second video with a thumbnail image of him with a gloved hand raised in the air post-fight. "I won that one."

She pressed on the two-minute video his manager at the time had made. It was from a fight almost eight years ago. It had only been his second ranked match, and he remembered feeling proud about the win.

"Jesus," Gwen said when the opponent struck him in the face.

The video wasn't linear; instead, it jumped from different moments in the twenty-four-minute fight with jarring techno music in the background.

"I can't imagine getting hit like this," she said, her eyes still glued to the screen. "Do you feel it when it's happening?"

"Adrenaline blocks most of it out," he said.

She suddenly turned off her phone. "Yeah, it's too much. I never could watch any of Duncan's fights either."

"It's not a pretty sport," he said, feeling her turn to face him.

"How many times have you broken your nose?" she asked.

"Six, I think," he said.

"'I think,'" she echoed with a small laugh before she

took a finger and lightly dragged it down the length of his broad nose.

The sound that emanated from him, a cross between a hiss and sigh, was stark in the quiet room.

She retracted her finger. "Sorry."

"No, it's okay," he said, his voice sounding too earnest, too revealing.

Silence hung between them, but he wondered if she could hear his heartbeat. She must.

He needed to turn his back to her and trick his brain into forgetting she was in bed with him. Maybe then he'd fall asleep.

But before Anthony could test out his theory, Gwen asked, "You know what I was thinking while you were lying in that hospital bed?"

"What?"

"How ridiculous it was that I lied about that kiss being meaningless," she said.

"What did it mean then?" he asked, not even trying to hide the strain in his voice.

"I don't know, but I've been thinking about it all week. How brief it was. How good it was."

Her words. Her sweet, sweet words were a lightning bolt shooting through him, and before he could think the wiser, he reached for her and brought their lips together.

It was like bathing in sunshine. Warm and gentle.

When their tongues met, the low moan that traveled from the depths of him could not be stopped. She tasted like mint, her skin covered in that intoxicating lavender scent he was obsessed with, and she felt so pliable under his hands.

He found her wide hips underneath the covers and drew her closer to him. The soft flesh of her breasts pressed against his chest, and he ached to feel her nipples harden in his mouth.

He let his lips travel along her cheek and across her beautiful jaw to give himself a break from the kisses that would surely lead him to do more than he intended. His journey took him down her neck, where he felt her rapid pulse.

"Tony," she said, sounding breathy and far away.

God, how he wanted to hear her say his name with more conviction, perhaps screaming it into his chest as he fucked her relentlessly. But he couldn't do that. That would be setting him up for the worst kind of post-sex regret.

This kissing was what he would do. What he could manage. All he'd allow himself.

As he made his way to her lips again, she took a hold of the back of his head and said, "Make me feel good."

————

Gwen knew it was the darkness that was making her so bold.

She'd had every intention of not kissing Tony again. It wasn't what she should be focused on at the moment. Not to mention, her request for him to make her feel good was a lot. She wasn't even sure what she meant by it.

Maybe this was a bad idea. He was injured, after all, and she had work tomorrow, and there was also—

"Get on your back," he said.

Her heart rattled at the sound of his voice, commanding but gentle.

She did what he told her, and was met with a kiss that deepened quickly. All the while, his hand slid underneath her shirt and cupped her bare breast, kneading and teasing her nipple to a stiff point with his fingers. A flutter settled in her stomach and spread across her body, leaving her feeling hot and impatient.

She needed more, and it was as if he could read her mind because his hand left her breast and skated down her stomach until it reached the waistband of her pajama bottoms. Her breath stilled as she waited for him to continue, but he just remained there, caressing her lower abdomen.

"What're you doing?" she asked, looking at him in the darkness.

"Giving you a chance to change your mind," he said.

She was practically vibrating with anticipation. "I'm not changing my mind."

A sound that hailed from somewhere deep in his chest escaped, and his hand, indelicate and large, slipped into her pants and firmly cupped her pussy. He simply held it for a second, and she felt ready to unravel from that alone.

When he started moving his rough hand slowly up and down, all she could do was look up at the dark ceiling and remember to breathe.

"This is what you're doing in the middle of the night? Getting yourself off? Touching this pussy?"

"Yes," she said on a moan.

"So it's my job tonight? To get you wet, make you come?"

She nodded.

Not in a million years and with a hundred guesses would she have ever thought she would be in this position with Tony. His dirty words in her ear and capable fingers working themselves up and down her slit.

She reached for him, wanting to make him feel as good as well, but he stopped her when she grazed the bulge at the front of his sweats.

"This will go a different way if you touch me," he said, kissing her cheek. "Just focus on coming for me."

She couldn't even protest because his fingers had zeroed on her clit, making her thoughts incoherent and jumbled. The rhythm was intoxicating. Not enough pressure to make her climax, but she felt herself slowly sliding into oblivion.

It was all-consuming.

Turning her head, she recaptured his lips in a kiss, and when he slipped his middle finger inside her, she moaned into his mouth, and her legs fell wide open.

"I know my dick would feel so good in here," he whispered, his voice strained as he continued to pump his finger inside her.

He buried his head in the crook of her neck, and she felt his tongue and teeth against her skin, notching her closer and closer.

"Make me come, please," she whimpered.

The words were no sooner out of her mouth than Tony was driving into her with purpose, and each time the heel of his hand made contact with her clit in the most electrifying way.

"Fuck," she said breathlessly as she grabbed onto his thigh lest she left her body. "Tony!"

"Right here, baby," he said against her face. "Come all over my fingers." There was so much going on and so many sensations coursing through her body, but she surrendered to them all.

With sweat on her brow, she felt herself nearing the end. She gripped the sheets as her hips bucked upward in response to Tony's continuing thrusts. And when he slipped a second finger into her, she felt the bright zap of her orgasm hit her. She slammed her eyes shut and rode the wave with a moan and floaty bits of light.

Chapter Twelve

WHEN ANTHONY WOKE up the next morning, he sprang up in bed thinking he'd missed his alarm, but the dull pain across his body quickly reminded him of all the events of the previous day… and night.

He whipped his head to the spot beside him and found it empty. Lowering himself back onto the pillow, he swung his arm across his face.

Fuck. Last night.

Gwen had fallen asleep almost immediately after coming. And thank God for that because heaven knows what he'd have done if she'd so much as insinuated wanting to do more. Instead, with his fingers still wet from teasing her to a climax, he'd left the room and gotten himself off in the bathroom. Picturing it was Gwen he was thrusting into rather than his hand.

When he'd returned to bed, he'd countered the urge to pull her to his chest by turning his back to her and willing himself to fall asleep. But just as he'd been about to drift off, Gwen's arm had flopped around his waist, and her leg hooked over his thigh. From her even breathing caressing his neck, he'd known she was still dead asleep.

It took him several more minutes to relax into her embrace, but when he did, he fell into the most blissful sleep he'd had in ages.

Anthony was yanked out of his musings by his vibrating phone, and he palmed for it on the side table and found a number of texts. The most recent one was from Ms. Katherine, letting him know she'd be at the apartment in the evening with a pot of soup for him. The rest of the messages were from the trainers at the gym, wishing him well. There was also a text Duncan had sent Anthony swearing to throttle him if he showed his face in Spotlight today.

His friend knew him well. It was tempting to disregard the doctor's orders, but Anthony would be helping no one by aggravating his injury. So R&R for the next few days it was.

Getting up, he made the bed and took a shower, noting improvement in the pain and his mobility. Afterward, he cooked himself a frittata, something he never had time to do, and sat at the bar counter to eat it.

Every other bite, he'd marvel at the novelty of this leisurely breakfast. He played some music on his phone to round out the experience and vowed to find room in his schedule for more mornings like this. That is, until he caught the time on the stove.

His first class of the day was happening at that very moment.

It was one of the advanced ones. Those classes typi-cally had regulars, and he worried that his substitute wouldn't use the playlist with no expletives if Connie was in class today. He'd also promised another client that he'd give him a list of good martial arts schools in the city for his teen.

The food turned bland in Anthony's mouth, and he eyed his phone, trying to weigh how annoying a call to the studio outlining how he'd like his classes conducted would be.

He needed to distract himself.

Once he'd scarfed down the remainder of his breakfast, he planted himself in front of the TV and started flipping through channels. He stopped when he landed on that morning show Gwen liked.

"Have you ever thought to yourself, 'How can I light as many Bath & Body Works candles as humanly possible without creating a fire hazard?'" the host asked. "Well, our next guest is going to show us how to do just that."

What ensued was a silly segment that had Anthony shaking his head, but he didn't reach for the remote for some reason. Instead, he sat there watching the two hosts talk in excruciating detail about candles with their guests. Apparently, based on his personality type, he needed to pick up some eucalyptus candles.

While the show held his attention for a little bit, he resumed compulsively checking the time. He might've eventually cracked and headed to the gym if Duncan hadn't shown up at the apartment two game shows and a bag of burnt popcorn later.

"This is for you," his friend said, handing Anthony a Starbucks cup the moment he stepped inside.

"Pumpkin spice," Anthony said, reading the order sticker.

"Too soon?"

"Yes, and disgusting," Anthony said after taking a sip of the unbearably sweet drink. He abandoned the cup on

the table and feigned nonchalance as he asked, "Everything's good at the gym?"

"Yeah, everything's running smoothly. Regina and
Trevor are splitting your classes for the first half of the
week."

Anthony nodded. He didn't know what he expected. It
wasn't like if Duncan had said everything had gone to hell
he could've suited up and gone to teach a high-impact
boxing class.

"You good?" Duncan asked.

Anthony knew he wasn't asking about how he was
doing physically.

"I don't know how to be idle," he replied dejectedly.

The last few weeks he'd been pushing himself to leave
his comfort zone for the sake of the gym's promotional
efforts. It had been a draining endeavor, heightened by the
fact that he felt out of control because of his living situation and the losing battle he was facing with his attraction
to Gwen.

In short, he felt vulnerable, like he'd been flayed open
and set out to bake in the sun.

"I get it. That's why I brought"—Duncan hoisted a
tote bag he'd been carrying onto the center table in the
living room—"entertainment."

"What's in there?"

Duncan pulled out the first item, a DVD boxset. "You
keep saying you're going to watch *Game of Thrones*. Now's
your chance. I also have a couple of books in there, some
snacks, and the business laptop if you feel like doing some
work."

"Jesus," Anthony said, peeking further into the bag.
"This is a lot, but thanks, man."

"Well, whatever keeps you from showing your mug at
the gym before your rest days are up."

———

The whirring drone of the cappuccino machines and the smell of sweet desserts were Gwen's lifeline after a hectic day. She sat across from Raven, sharing a plate of chocolate chip cookies at a coffee shop two blocks from the school.

"How's Tony doing?" Raven asked. "I was going to text you last night, but I thought you probably had enough to deal with."

"He's fine. Doing great. Very well," Gwen said as she kept her gaze on the cookie she was eating.

"Wait. What's that tone?"

"What?" Gwen asked.

"You get all high-pitched when you're hiding something."

Gwen looked up at her friend and hesitated before saying, "He slept in my bed."

"He slept in your bed? Okay. Where did you sleep?"

"My bed."

"You both slept in your bed?"

"Correct."

"All right," Raven said as she picked up her cell. "I'm going to turn my phone on Do Not Disturb, then you're going to tell me what the hell is going on."

Gwen leaned back in her seat and let out a long exhale. "It was all an accident. We couldn't get the sofa bed out, so I offered my bed. One thing led to another, and we fooled around."

Her friend's mouth opened on a silent squeal. "What did I say about sync—"

"Don't you dare say 'synchronous,'" Gwen said before closing her eyes for a moment. "It was such a bad idea, Ray."

"How! Why?"

"Because now I'm all distracted. I can't get him out of my head. I spent fifteen minutes thinking about whether or not to leave him a thank-you note this morning. I wrote like five versions before realizing I was doing too much."

Gwen had hoped that last night would've abated her attraction. But she'd woken up with her limbs around him and the desire to bury herself more firmly against his body.

"I have a suggestion, but I'm pretty sure you'll hate it," Raven said.

"What is it?"

"Maybe," her friend said slowly, "you need to pull the trigger and, you know, actually sleep with him. Get it out of your system."

"You're right, I hate it."

Gwen refused to complicate things unnecessarily. This was her brother's best friend, after all. That was a category she'd like to keep him in. It was neater that way. Less complicated. She much preferred crossing paths with past hookups in the produce section at the grocery store, not over spiked eggnog at an annual holiday party.

"It could be like a juice cleanse of sorts," Raven said.

"The first and last cleanse I tried left me hungry and with sweat that smelled like celery, so no thanks."

"Fine. Bad analogy, but I think the sex could be a sort of reset for you. It would get you back on track with finding Mr. Right with those matchmakers you so adore."

God, the matchmakers. She'd already postponed her date that night for later in the week, and she'd convinced herself it was because she was tired. But the truth was she didn't think she would be very good company if she were constantly drifting off into la-la land to think about the big hands that had her moaning at one in the morning.

But she didn't need a "reset."

"I'm not some out-of-control robot," Gwen said.

Raven lifted her hands in surrender. "What are you going to do?"

"Simply force my lust into submission."

"Oh," Raven said, laughing. "I'm sure that'll go well."

———

Early in the evening, Old Man Enoch and Ms. Katherine showed up to the apartment using the directions Anthony had sent them. And as promised, they arrived bearing a pot full of soup they said would "warm him right up." Their presence immediately lifted Anthony's mood.

"What a charming apartment," Ms. Katherine said as they entered. "Nancy Myers on a budget."

"What time do you usually expect Gwen?" Enoch asked.

"Oh, we should wait for her," Ms. Katherine said, her eyes brightening.

"Her schedule isn't that defined," Anthony said quickly.

For all he knew, she could be on a date tonight. The thought made his stomach roll. He didn't want to think of her sitting across from some asshole in a bowtie.

"Okay, we'll wait for a little while. If she doesn't show, we'll eat," Ms. Katherine said.

So they sat in Gwen's living room as Enoch dramatized the long-winded statement Cheating Jeremy had posted after his Giant Pumpkin Weigh-off loss.

All the while, Anthony tried not to anticipate Gwen's return. But he couldn't ignore how his heart leaped when the front door eventually opened.

"Aye! You're home," Enoch said to Gwen, who'd frozen at the door, taking in the scene in her apartment.

Her face broke out into a smile a second later. "Nice to see you two again so soon."

"Sorry to barge in like this. We wanted to bring Anthony dinner," Ms. Katherine said.

"Oh, it's no problem," Gwen said.

Gwen and Tony's eyes briefly met as she shrugged out of her coat. She gave him a small nod, but you'd think she'd given him a wink and beckoned him closer with her finger the way he failed to breathe for a second.

"It smells really good," Gwen said, entering the kitchen and looking into the pot that Ms. Katherine had placed on the stove to keep warm.

"Carrot, sweet potato, and ginger soup," Enoch said. "With rosemary focaccia."

"There's more than enough for everyone," Ms. Katherine said.

The kitchen got crowded as everyone took turns washing their hands and getting bowls and utensils.

"Sorry about this," Anthony said to Gwen quietly.

Her eyebrows shot up in question.

Anthony nodded toward the old couple who were debating about the best spoon shape to eat soup with.

"No, it's okay. They're sweet and entertaining," Gwen said. "How are you feeling, by the way?"

"Not bad," he said, before adding, "Spent the day watching a lot of talk shows."

"Sounds to me like you're really living the life," she said.

"All for the small, small price of a nudge from a giant autumnal vegetable," he replied, and the dimpled smile she unleashed in response nearly bowled him over.

"The soup is getting cold!" Ms. Katherine said, urging them to hand over their bowls.

Once they'd all gotten their food, they squished into

Gwen's small living room to eat. Anthony sat on the end of the couch with Gwen right next to him. Their legs flush against each other, and he was just glad his hands were occupied.

"Sorry I don't have a real dining table for you to eat at," Gwen said.

"No, this is fine. Reminds me of the apartment Enoch and I lived in when we first got married," Ms. Katherine said.

"Oh, this place is much nicer," Enoch said. "Ours had roaches and leaky faucets."

"We had each other. That made things better," Ms. Katherine said.

Even as someone who didn't naturally lean into senti-ment, Anthony enjoyed listening to the older couple talk about their love.

"How did you two meet?" Gwen asked.

"You want to tell the story?" Ms. Katherine asked her husband.

"No, you go ahead, dear. You always give me a hard time about the details," he replied.

"You're right. I don't even know why I asked. Okay, so I'd just moved back to the city for a job, and he worked at the grocery store near my sister's place," Ms. Katherine said. "And, of course, I noticed him imme-diately."

Enoch smiled and dusted his shoulder and said, "What can I say? I was a catch with luscious hair."

"He sure was, and I was trying to build up the courage to just speak to him like the modern woman I thought I was."

"There were always so many people in that store that I never really paid attention to any one person. I just wanted to get through my shift and go home," Enoch said.

"Well, one day I saw him shining the apples that were on display right at the front—"

"They were stacked into a pyramid real high," Enoch explained.

Ms. Katherine nodded. "And I go up to him, thinking I'll casually start a conversation with him by asking about the apples. But the moment I pick one up, the pyramid crumbles."

Gwen gasped and covered a sudden laugh with her hand.

"And I'm ready to be pissed off, right," Enoch said, shifting forward in his seat. "It had taken me forever to build it, and now someone had just destroyed it. But then I see who the culprit is, and well, I asked her out to dinner instead."

"And the rest is history," Ms. Katherine declared.

"Ah! That is the sweetest story," Gwen said, beaming at the older couple.

"When did you two meet?" Ms. Katherine asked, gesturing her spoon between Anthony and Gwen.

"Oh, we're not together," Gwen said, looking over at Anthony, who felt his face heat up.

"Of course not," Ms. Katherine said quickly. "I'm just asking generally."

Gwen laughed a little and said, "I actually don't remember. Do you, Tony?"

"We met at Duncan's old place," Anthony said. "You showed up to get him to sign a birthday card for your grandmother."

Anthony had been friends with Duncan for a little over two years at that point, and he'd heard about Gwen in passing but never really thought much about her. But that day, when she'd breezed into her brother's apartment wearing a short dress and wedges, it stopped him dead.

She, on the other hand, didn't even notice him at first.

When Duncan had introduced them, she had smiled big and bright and firmly shook his hand. He'd barely made an impression on her, but it was the beginning of his long-held crush.

"Could be wrong, though," he said, returning to the current conversation.

"No, no, I vaguely remember that," Gwen replied.

When they finished their meals, Anthony and Old Man Enoch headed to the kitchen to serve the dessert.

The whole setup felt familiar and cozy as Gwen's warm laughter cascaded through the room.

He caught the old man looking at him.

"What's up?" Anthony asked.

"No, nothing," Enoch said, handing him the knife for the pie. "I was just thinking how sweet it is that you let her call you Tony."

Anthony turned to the older man. "What?"

"You let her call you Tony. I don't think I've ever heard anyone call you that."

Anthony shrugged. "It's a variation of my name."

Even to Anthony's own ears, his tone sounded defensive.

It was true; he never let anyone call him Tony. He never felt like the name suited him. But the name on Gwen's tongue didn't sound so foreign or grating.

"Just a light comment, son," Enoch said as he picked up the plates Anthony had just placed pie slices on. "Don't think too hard about it."

But that's exactly what he'd do.

Chapter Thirteen

AFTER A LOVELY DINNER and long evening of conversation, Ms. Katherine and Mr. Enoch left Gwen's apartment. Tony followed right behind them; he'd insisted on walking them to their vehicle.

The solitude gave Gwen time to gather her thoughts. Tonight had proven something to her. Raven was right: she needed to get this attraction to Tony out of her system.

After boldly declaring she'd be able to bring her lust into submission, it was an embarrassing conclusion for her to admit. But once she got it over and done with, she was sure she could throw herself back into her matchmaking commitments.

The entire evening she couldn't help but steal glances at him or feel the flutter in her stomach every time their limbs accidentally touched. It was no way to live.

She thought the simplest way of going about her plan was to do what she'd done last night and initiate something while they were lying in her bed in the dark. So Gwen slipped into the bathroom, took a shower, and brushed her teeth.

By the time she was in her room contemplating what to wear, Tony had returned and was getting ready for bed as well.

While the water pipes gurgled, she settled on wearing a pajama slip dress she tended to only pull out during warmer months, thinking it was at least sexier than a full flannel PJ set.

Quickly, she got into bed and sat up against her headboard before arranging her duvet over her lap and adjusting her boobs so they were positioned perfectly. She then picked up the book from her nightstand and waited.

Minutes passed before she realized the water from the shower was no longer running. She craned her neck to peer out of her bedroom door and saw that the bathroom was empty, but the lights in the front area of her apartment were still on.

He may be getting a drink of water, she reasoned.

But several more minutes elapsed and he'd still not walked in, so Gwen slinked out of her bedroom to investigate. She tiptoed into the living room, unsure what she'd find. When she saw Tony sitting on top of his unfurled bed, on his laptop, her heart sank.

"I didn't realize you'd managed to pull out the bed," she said when he turned to look at her.

She eyed the couch as if it had personally betrayed her.

"Yeah, it wasn't too difficult tonight."

"That's great!" she said, trying to mean it. "Well, I'll head to bed then. Have a good night."

She'd spend the minutes before she drifted off to sleep wallowing in self-pitying horniness.

"Gwen," Tony called out before she could make it down the hallway.

Whipping back around a little too eagerly, Gwen watched as he got up and approached her. He wore a white T-shirt and some dark sweatpants, but he might as well have been naked and greased up in oil.

Her mouth grew drier with every step he took.

"Your phone," he said when he reached her. "It was between the seat cushions."

Gwen looked down at his outstretched hand that held her cell, feeling a wave of annoyance at herself.

"Thank you," she said.

As she reached for the phone, their hands brushed, and it was as if someone struck a resonant chord. A vibration zipped through her entire body, and time stood still as they looked at each other. How had she known him for so many years and not turned into mush in his presence before?

"You know, you're very distracting," she whispered.

The succeeding silence crackled between them, and she thought they'd remain standing there forever with her words going unacknowledged.

But Tony took a step forward, she let out a sharp exhale, and that was it.

The space between them vanished, and they were all over each other.

He smelled of that cheap soap he kept in the shower. That was the first thing she registered when his arms wrapped around her in a cocoon of a hold. The kiss was as searing and discombobulating as all the previous ones, and she fell headfirst into the feeling.

In a few smooth steps, he had her pinned up against the hallway wall with his hands skimming her body. It felt so good to let go. To cease the mental work of deluding herself that this wasn't exactly what she wanted.

When she slipped her hands underneath his T-shirt to feel the hard surface of his torso, a grunt, deep and bold, left his lips, nurturing the ache between her legs.

His mouth traveled along her face and down her neck,

and the little air in her lungs expelled as his fingers massaged the flesh of her upper thighs.

"Me, a distraction?" he asked against her throat. "You're the one with the tight pussy I can't stop thinking about."

"Yeah?" she asked, deliriously turned on and unable to give him anything but breathy, needy responses.

When her frenetic hands finally made contact with the impressive bulge at the front of his pants, Tony's grip on her tightened and his breath hitched.

He pressed his lips to hers once again and pushed up the flimsy material of her slip to palm her bare ass. She thought he might finger-fuck her or take her right there against the wall, but with disorienting swiftness, he moved them to the back of the sofa.

"Bend over," he said, his eyes ablaze and his expression fierce.

Her clit hummed with anticipation as she turned around and folded her body over the back of the couch with her ass in the air and eyes forward, looking into her living room.

All she could hear was the blood pumping in her ears and harsh breathing she didn't know for sure was hers or Tony's or both.

He flipped the fabric of her silk dress up around her waist and then lowered himself to his knees. When he pushed her legs apart, she thought she might've whimpered. There was no doubt he could see how wet she was.

"Fuck, Gwen," he said, his voice gruff and strained.

His lips and hands brushed against the back of her thighs, and at that moment, she was grateful for the couch underneath that held her up. He traveled up her leg, kissing and caressing her skin, and when he reached the apex of her thighs, she didn't have even a moment to prepare herself before he buried his face against her pussy.

The desperate moan that left her mouth echoed through the room, and with the first warm stroke of his tongue, all she could do was hold on for dear life. He firmly gripped her hips, keeping her in place as he continued to move his tongue and mouth all over her. Her heart beat fast and sweat peppered her skin, and she was edging to a climax faster than she could ever recall experiencing.

But she couldn't come now.

If this was the one and only time she could feel Tony tongue-fucking her into incoherence, then she needed to savor it, burn it in her memory. She'd use the mental image to get herself off for years to come.

Her plan, however, was sabotaged the moment Tony's fingers found her clit.

"Oh, fuck me," she breathlessly said, reaching back to seize his curly hair in her fist. The combination of his rough hands and his soft wet tongue was heaven on earth. His responding low moans reverberated through her.

She was so close. Her eyes grew heavy, and she couldn't make up from down. And as a final gift, Tony teased her back entrance with the pad of his finger, and it launched her into dazzling variegated light.

―――

Anthony was watching the most stunning woman take his dick into her mouth. If it weren't for the way his balls tightened every time Gwen swirled her perfect tongue around his tip, he might think he was dreaming. There was also the fact that he could still taste her on his lips and hear her sublime cries of pleasure ringing in his ears.

"Look at me," he choked out.

A flutter in his chest took flight as her big brown eyes flicked upward to meet his gaze, and he almost regretted asking her to do it.

He was trying to keep his mind focused solely on physical pleasure. But when she looked at him with an intense but flirtatious glint, all he wanted to do was repeatedly declare how incredible she was and caress her cheek as she took increasingly more of him between her lips.

"That's it, baby," he said, his head falling back for a moment as the contours of her mouth tightened around him.

This woman. This fucking woman.

"Such a pretty mouth sucking me off," he said, taking hold of her head to guide her faster over his dick.

She planted her hands on his thighs to brace herself, and he continued to pump into her until he felt himself slip too close to a climax. He pulled his dick from her mouth and hoisted her to her feet. That couldn't be the first place he came.

"You okay?" she asked, slightly breathless.

For a moment, he had no idea why she'd ask such a question and look so concerned like she hadn't just given him the most incredible head, but then he remembered. He was still supposed to be recovering. Five to six days of no rigorous activity.

He'd all but forgotten about it, and he didn't give a shit about the pain that might hit him in the morning.

"I'm good," he whispered before kissing her deeply, and that damn flutter in his chest made a reappearance when she wrapped her arms around his neck.

Slowly and without ever losing contact, they found their way onto Anthony's bed. She maneuvered him onto his back and straddled his hips before peppering his chest and arms with kisses. God, he couldn't wait to be inside her.

"Protection," she said.

Anthony reached over the side of his bed for the back pocket in his duffle bag, thanking every saint and deity that he always kept a few condoms on hand.

While Gwen finally did away with the shiny black dress she still wore, he rolled the condom over his dick. When their lips met once again, he pulled her onto his lap.

His hands roamed her body, first squeezing her hard nipples between his fingers, before caressing her soft torso on his way to grip the flesh on her hips. Again, he marveled at the sight of her.

"Tell me if I hurt you," she said.

He'd rather die.

She planted a hand on his chest and slowly lowered herself down his length. They both let out sounds from somewhere deep within.

With her head tipped back, she said, "God, you're so…"

She sat there for a while, and he forced himself to stay still until she was ready. And just as he thought he might actually lose it, she started a slow ascent on his dick before coming back down just as methodically. There was a breathy hitch that escaped her lips every time she got to the hilt. Like she was shocked that she made it all the way. Watching his dick reappear and disappear into her slick folds had Anthony seeing stars and spots of light in his vision.

"God, you're so beautiful," he said.

As she picked up speed, the sound of her ass slapping against his thighs as she came down intermingled with their desperate moans and gasps. The pain that sliced through him as she dug her fingernails into his chest shot straight to his balls, and he tightened his hold on her hips and started meeting her downward movements with thrusts.

"Tony! Tony! Tony!" she chanted, and his heart pressed violently against his chest. This was his dream girl. The woman he'd spent years infatuated with, and here she was losing herself in the pleasure he was providing her.

"You like this dick?" he asked, his voice rough and possibly too loud.

She nodded as pleasure gripped her features. "Every. Fucking. Inch."

He increased the power of his thrusts, and she moved her hand to her pussy to rub and tease her clit. Anthony could barely see straight, but he committed the way she looked at that moment to memory.

Suddenly, she grabbed one of his hands that held her hips and brought it to her neck, and something inside him shifted when she sighed in response to the gentle pressure he applied around her throat.

"I'm gonna come," she whispered.

"All I want, baby," he said as he continued to pump into her. She suddenly slumped onto his chest, and he breathed in her scent, licking and kissing the soft skin on her neck. As his climax neared, he willed himself to hold off until she got hers.

"That's it. Come for me," he said as her pussy tightened around him and her body began to shake.

She grabbed onto his biceps and let out a long low moan that set him off immediately. He wrapped his arms around her waist and came thrusting into her, grunting sweet, inarticulate words.

Chapter Fourteen

ANTHONY DIDN'T KNOW if he could do it anymore. On the third day of his mandatory rest period, a boredom like he'd never experienced settled over. He'd really thought he'd make it to the end. After all, he had all the entertainment he needed and even found the perfect spot in the apartment where the WiFi wasn't dodgy so he could complete some admin work.

But still, he'd grown impatient, and when he woke up on the fourth day, he decided he was ready to go back to work.

Getting up, he headed to the washroom to prepare for the day ahead and stepped into the hallway just as Gwen was leaving her room, dressed in a big sweater and dark trousers.

"Good morning!" she said, with a smile that stopped his heart for a beat.

"Morning."

He realized it had been foolish to believe that sleeping with her two nights ago would diminish his attraction to her. Instead, it had intensified. Now he was plagued by it.

Eyes shut or wide awake, thoughts of Gwen weren't far behind. She, on the other hand, seemed content with their one sexual encounter and had been cordial and breezy since.

"I've gotta go," she said, gesturing at the front door.

"Me too," he said, pointing to the bathroom, but then he realized it sounded like he was saying he needed to take a shit, so he added, "First day back at the gym. Don't want to be late, you know?"

"Oh, today?"

"Yeah, I feel strong," he said, and to his utter shame, he instinctively flexed his biceps like some show pony.

He wanted to launch his head into the drywall.

"That's great! Have a good first day back," she said with the lightest touch to his shoulder before leaving the apartment with her work bags.

A slew of incoming texts prevented him from running the interaction over and over in his head, but when he saw all of the messages were from Duncan, he ignored them. His friend was likely pissed off about the email Anthony had sent at the crack of dawn announcing his comeback.

He would not be dissuaded.

When he finally arrived at Spotlight an hour later, he only narrowly ignored the urge to drop to his knees and kiss the floor.

He walked past the empty foyer and headed to the staff room where his team was chatting and prepping for the morning.

"Hey, boss!" a trainer named Joshua said when the room finally noticed him. "Didn't expect you for a couple more days."

"How're you feeling?" another team member asked, standing up to pull out a chair for him.

Anthony graciously waved off the offer to take a seat

and said, "Good. Nothing was broken, so I feel ready to get back to work."

"Well, shit. Welcome back then," Joshua said just as Duncan entered the room.

"You haven't answered my messages all morning," his business partner said, his expression pinched and his arms crossed.

"That was on purpose," Anthony said, patting Duncan on the back.

"Anthony—"

"I feel fine. I don't need any more rest."

But from the look on Duncan's face, Anthony felt his friend had some sort of plan to force him to complete his doctor-sanctioned rest. So he quickly slipped past him and out of the staff room.

"Where are you—"

"Got some things to do before my first class," Anthony said, making a beeline for the office.

He'd barricade himself in there until it was time to teach, but his plan was subverted when Duncan forced his way past the door.

"Will you stop running and listen to me?" Duncan said, grabbing him by the shoulders. "I'm trying to tell you something."

Anthony sighed. "What?"

Duncan hadn't formulated more than two words before Milo burst into the room and said, "You've gone viral."

"*That*," Duncan said, letting his head flop back.

Anthony blinked. "What?"

"You," the social media manager said, pointing at Anthony. "Have. Gone. Viral."

"H-how? Why?" Anthony asked, his brain scrambling to make sense of the words being hurled at him.

Milo scurried over and pulled out his phone.

"Someone filmed you saving those two kids from that giant pumpkin over the weekend."

"Are you serious?" Anthony asked as he watched the shaky footage of him from the Fall Harvest Festival.

There was a whole lot more chaos and noise than he'd remembered, and it was no wonder the kids couldn't hear him. Also, when he'd dove to push the two children out of the way, he could've sworn it looked more athletic than what it appeared on screen. He looked like a drunk baseball player diving into home plate.

"So you're saying this video is being shared," Anthony said slowly.

"Yes, but don't get too excited. You're not like trending on Twitter or anything, and I don't think Jimmy Kimmel is gonna give you a call, but you've got some traction on Reddit," Milo said.

"Some traction on Reddit," Anthony said as if repeating the words would reveal what all the fuss was about.

"Yeah, like a couple thousand upvotes and comments," Milo said. "And it's also having a little moment on Facebook. Particularly with mom-centric groups."

Duncan nodded, grinning. "They're calling you a hero and brave and—"

"A Knight in Sweaty Under Armour," Milo said.

Anthony looked between the two men, noting that he didn't feel a quarter of their enthusiasm.

"Well, I guess I can check 'go viral' off my bucket list then."

As he moved to sit at the desk, Milo darted in his path and said, "Wait, wait, don't you see? This is perfect. Exactly what we need."

"What do we need?" Anthony asked.

"Fifteen minutes of fame. You have to take it and do something with it," Milo said, his eyes practically glowing.

Anthony looked at Duncan to see if he could maybe translate, but his friend just shrugged.

"Think big picture, guys," Milo said as he began to pace the room. "I know I'm your social media coordinator and not a PR person, but this situation can totally be spun to benefit the gym. If we start today by making it known that it's you in the video, we could..."

Milo's words were coming out too fast and too earnestly for Anthony to feel anything but a slow pulse of anxiety. He couldn't capitalize on his near-death experience. Could he?

"Can we have a minute, Milo?" Duncan asked.

Milo froze, looked at the gym owners, and said, "Sure, okay. Yeah, discuss it amongst yourselves. See if it's something that works for you guys, and we'll go from there."

Once he'd left the room, Duncan asked Anthony, "Where's your head at?"

"I don't know. It's a wild situation."

"Listen, man, don't feel pressure to turn this into some opportunity for Spotlight. We're good. Slow and steady."

"But it *could* help us if we play our cards right," Anthony said heavily.

"Yeah, maybe. Or it could fizzle out by noon."

"That's even more reason to try," Anthony said.

"It's one hundred percent up to you. I'll support either way."

The two friends stood there as Anthony let the idea percolate. There could be some unpleasantness that could come from dropping his guard a little and embracing virality. But he could also envision the upsides: Spotlight's phone ringing off the hook with clients trying to get into already booked classes, future franchise opportunities, an office with better lighting.

"Milo!" Anthony called out suddenly.

"Yes?" the social media manager said, popping his head back in.

Anthony sighed before asking, "Where do we start?"

———

The music was too loud.

Gwen couldn't really hear her date, a sweet guy named Rami who worked in finance. She was watching his mouth move, and while she nodded and smiled, she hadn't a clue what he was saying.

He had nice teeth, though.

She shouldn't be on this date anyway. To her disappointment, her brain was still muddled and focused on Tony. It had been that way for days now. So much for getting it out of her system, because she wanted more. A lot more. Harder. Slower. In the shower. On top of a table. Wherever he'd take her.

But she'd promised herself that she'd get back into dating once she'd slept with him, and that's what she was doing. She was also motivated to refocus on her love life because she'd received an email from her matchmaker with the subject line, "Very important update."

She was terrified to open it. For some reason, she felt a scolding was waiting for her or, worse, a notice that she'd been thrown out of the program for recently being a subpar and unengaging dater.

"Sorry!" Gwen shouted to Rami over the bass-heavy music when she realized he'd just asked her a question. "I didn't catch that."

"I said, do you have to deal with a lot of drama as a teacher?"

"No, not really. The most dramatic thing is probably a kid throwing up."

"Gnarly!"

"Yeah, it's bound to happen, though. Pop-Tarts and neon drinks are a good portion of their diets."

Rami laughed before snapping his fingers and said, "Speaking of…"

The tail end of what he said was eclipsed by the noise, but he handed her his phone and shouted, "You have to watch this video!"

"What is it?" Gwen asked.

"A heroic feat for the ages," Rami said. "A guy saved these kids from a pumpkin. It was at some place a half hour outside of the city…"

Rami's voice faded along with everything else as Gwen watched a shaky video of Tony's bravery the other day. Her mouth fell open as the rescue unfold on screen. She was in awe of Tony's agility, speed, and fearlessness.

It was kinda hot.

"I know him," Gwen said once the video had looped.

"What?" Rami asked.

"He's my roommate. Kind of."

"Shit. Really?"

"Yeah. I was actually there that day."

"Jesus. What was it like?" her date asked, leaning forward.

"It all happened so fast. I didn't even register what was going on until people were surrounding his body."

"Huh," Rami said before springboarding off into a conversation about studies on eyewitness reliability.

Meanwhile, Gwen was fighting to maintain the little interest she had for the dinner date when all she wanted to do was watch the video again and read what people had to say.

She got her chance an hour later when she arrived home, and while she rode the elevator to her floor, she scrolled through the comments. The reception fell into three buckets:

(1) Genuine, heartfelt ones:
   "Do people still do #ManCrushMondays because…"
   "THIS is a hero!!"

(2) Memes and jokes:
   "When I cancel a subscription on the last day of the free trial."
   "The future pumpkin spice latte lovers want."

(3) Skepticism:
   "Sus AF! Totally staged."
   "The video is faker than my orgasms with my ex."

When she entered her apartment, the TV was on, and Tony was in the kitchen making a peanut butter and jelly sandwich.

"You're famous," she said when he looked up.

"Famous is a strong word," he replied flatly.

"Why does your nonchalance not surprise me?" she asked as she came to stand in the kitchen with him.

Big strong hero, and he didn't even care to bask in the adoration just a little bit.

"I think people are just bored," he said.

"Or endeared by a selfless act," she countered.

"Hmm. Do you want one?" he asked of the sandwiches on his plate he'd just finished constructing.

"Maybe just half," she said. "I already had dinner."

He seemed to realize that "dinner" meant date, but he didn't probe. She watched him cut one of the sandwiches down the middle and offer it to her on a plate.

"It's tragic you cut sandwiches this way," she said, taking one rectangle.

"How are you supposed to cut it?"

"Into triangles," she said.

"Is that a rule or something?" he asked.

She nodded. "In the Bible and everything."

Tony huffed before picking up the knife again and diagonally cutting the other untouched sandwich. He then took the piece she'd already bitten into and swapped it with the correctly shaped one.

"There," he said.

"Better. Thank you," she said, smiling.

They ate their respective sandwiches in silence for a while before Gwen asked, "What does going viral feel like?"

"Like when you get a coupon but then realize it's expired," he said.

"Oh, shit."

"But our social media manager thinks we could take advantage of this little attention, at least locally. Might do the gym some good."

"Like going on the radio or something?" she asked.

"TV," he said with a small smile.

"Why are you smiling?" she asked.

He didn't say anything, but his smile grew incrementally, and Gwen studied him for a second longer before it suddenly clicked.

"You're going to be on *Cup of Joe*!" she said, her voice high and verging on pitchy.

"Yeah. It was a—"

"Stop," she said, picking up then tossing a dish towel from the counter at him. "You're going to be on *Cup of Joe Morning Show*?"

Now he was laughing, a deep but subtle sound that was one of the most glorious things she'd heard in a while.

"When?" she asked.

"Day after tomorrow. I think."

"I'm trying very hard not to be jealous," she said.

"I'd give you a C-plus on that account," he said with a playful tilt of his head.

"Holy crap! Are you nervous?"

"No. As long as I can string some sentences together and not have bad breath, I'll be fine," he said.

"They like guests who compliment them, and Hayley appreciates when people mention her charity work. It allows her to plug it on the show."

"I'll try and remember that," he said, sticking his thumb in his mouth to remove peanut butter.

She watched the slow movement, easily recalling the night when his capable tongue was all over her body.

Her gaze must've been projecting everything she was thinking because Tony stilled.

She had to get out of there because if he said her name in that addicting timbre of his, her legs would be around his waist.

"I should head to bed. Thanks for the triangle sandwich," she said, grateful her voice didn't sound airy and lust-filled. However, with each step she took toward her room, she felt like she was dragging cinder blocks behind her.

———

Anthony didn't let ten seconds pass without looking at the python draped around the neck of the man sitting beside him.

They were both in the green room for the *Cup of Joe Morning Show*. The man, a zookeeper, had been invited to showcase a gaggle of exotic animals.

"Just be yourself," Duncan said, pulling Anthony back to the video call he was on.

"Yes, of course. And what matters is on the inside, and all we need is love," Anthony responded.

"Okay, I'm going to ignore the sarcasm because I know you're nervous."

Anthony sighed. He'd told Gwen he wasn't worried about the interview, but sometime between then and now, he'd grown a little edgy. Spotlight was one of the good things in his life, and he'd hate to harm the business by coming off unlikeable on TV.

"You'll be fine, man," Duncan said. "I've seen you do scarier things before."

Anthony turned over the Tic Tac container in his hand that Gwen had left on the counter that morning for him. It had been accompanied with a note that read, "For the bad breath. Good luck!" It had actually made him laugh out loud.

The guest coordinator for the show appeared in the room then, prompting Anthony to end his call with Duncan and stand up. She ushered him past fast-walking people with headsets and clipboards onto the stage with shockingly bright lights that made him feel hot almost immediately.

He took a seat on a chair when instructed and tried to arrange his body in a way that read casual and friendly.

"Remember, no need to look directly into the cameras. Just at Hayley and Russell," the coordinator said, pointing toward the hosts that were on the other side of the stage on their phones.

"Sounds good," he said as he ran his hand across his forehead, forgetting the makeup an artist had applied an hour ago.

Before he could ask the coordinator if he'd messed with the makeup, she'd disappeared, and someone in the unseeable abyss past the stage shouted, "Quiet on set! We're live in five, four…"

And by the time Anthony straightened in his seat, the studio audience was clapping and the hosts had put away their phones and produced show-stopping smiles with the biggest, straightest, whitest teeth.

"Welcome back, everybody," Hayley said with cloying energy. "We've been teasing our next guest all morning. Have you seen this video of a man leaping in to save two small children from a runaway giant pumpkin?"

The footage of Anthony's rescue played on the big screen behind the hosts. The audience gasped at the part where the pumpkin split open and spilled its stringy guts.

"Hayley, I have to be honest and say I've watched this video so many times, I could probably reenact it for you," Russell said.

The audience laughed.

"Well, that won't be necessary, Russell. Not only because I don't know if your insurance will cover the physiotherapy you'd need, but also because in the studio today with us, we've got the real hero from the video, who just so happens to be from our great city."

With those words, Anthony felt every eyeball and camera lens turn to him. His heart was pounding, and he was thankful he'd opted for a dark shirt that would mask sweat stains.

"Anthony Woods, how are you?" Hayley asked.

He opened his mouth, but nothing came out. He felt panic start to creep in, but he took a deep breath and steeled himself against it. This was no time to choke; he would not choke. It was game time.

"Good," Anthony replied after clearing his throat. "A little disappointed I won't get to see Russell's reenactment, though."

The hosts were delighted at his comeback, and so was the audience. It felt like landing a jab on an opponent who'd been slipping punches.

"How have the last few days been for you? This only happened not even a week ago, correct?" Russell asked.

"Yeah, on Sunday. And it's been surreal," he replied, remembering to smile.

"What were you thinking when you decided to jump in and save those children? You had to be scared," Hayley said.

"I didn't really think," Anthony said. "It was just instinct."

"Good on ya, mate!" Russell said with an undoubtedly practiced wink. "And does that instinct come from your training as a professional boxer?"

"I'm sure it helped," Anthony said.

"And you own a boxing gym, right? I can see the logo on that impressive chest of yours," Hayley said.

"Down, girl," Russell said with a saucy smile to the camera.

"Oh, shush, Russ. A few bench presses might get you there too," Hayley said, and the two hosts started laughing like bleating goats.

The rest of the interview was a blur for Anthony. It

wasn't until he was sitting in the living room that evening, watching the episode back with Gwen, that he even remembered half of what he'd said.

"Turn the volume up," Gwen said as she entered the room and settled beside him on the couch with a pint of ice cream and utensils.

"Your skin looks amazing," she said, cracking the cold dessert open and handing him a spoon.

"Lights and makeup," he said.

He hated watching himself, and it was Gwen's enthusiasm alone that had him suffering through it. She'd been waiting for him when he got home, and he hadn't had it in him to tell her that he'd prefer not to watch.

They were a dozen spoonfuls into the ice cream and halfway through his segment when Gwen said, "You know, ever since you told me about Russell's fake accent, I haven't been able to enjoy him the same way. He just comes off arrogant now."

"Sorry for destroying the fantasy," he said.

"No, I prefer the rose-tinted glasses off."

Anthony glanced over at her. The statement was too emphatic to be only about a random talk show host. It sounded like a life motto.

"Before we go," Hayley said, drawing Anthony's attention back to his interview playing out on the television screen, "I'd be remiss if I didn't ask about your love life. Are you single, Mr. Woods?"

"I knew she was going to ask that," Gwen said, pointing at the TV. "She was flirting with you earlier."

"That wasn't even the weirdest question I was asked," Anthony said.

"What do you mean?"

"Backstage, after everything, a producer approached

me and asked if I'd ever be interested in doing *I Choose You!*"

"Oh my God!" Gwen said, sitting straight and turning to face him.

The local morning talk show had a recurring thirty-minute segment called *I Choose You!* It was a dating game with a borrowed concept. Three singles, hidden behind a screen, would vie for the affection of an eligible romantic lead. The lead would ask a series of questions and, based on the answers, pick one person to take out.

"Are you gonna do it?" Gwen asked.

"Yeah, I just need to sign the contract, pick up my suit, and—No," he said as Gwen laughed.

The entire time the producer was explaining the segment to Anthony, he had had to resist looking over his shoulder to see who she was really talking to. Dating, in general, was already an awkward activity, so to do it in front of a nationwide audience seemed like his version of hell.

"For what it's worth, I think you'd be great at it," Gwen said.

He looked at her with raised eyebrows.

"You would!" she insisted. "You came off well on TV."

"As opposed to in real life."

She swatted his arm. "You know what I mean."

"I don't get why I would let a stranger pick other strangers for me to date," he said.

"It's not so different from what I'm doing with the matchmakers," she said, shrugging.

Anthony never liked thinking about Gwen's robust dating life, but one question had nagged him since finding out she'd hired the matchmaking service.

"Can I ask you something—and you can tell me if it's out of line or whatever," he said carefully.

She nodded for him to continue.

"Is it hard for you to date in real life? A matchmaker can't be cheap," he said.

"I don't have trouble dating, but I value compatibility. You know, because of my parents and their bullshit."

From the years Anthony had been friends with Duncan, he knew that the Gilmore parents had had a bad marriage. The kind where arguments were served as a side during dinnertime.

"I remember waking up one morning when I was thirteen with horrible stomach pain," Gwen said, staring at a spot in front of her. "I thought I'd finally started my period, but it was so severe that my mom had to take me to the clinic."

Anthony watched Gwen closely as she played with the fringe on the throw blanket across her lap.

"Turns out I had developed an ulcer. I'd been so anxious and stressed about their fighting that my body just sorta rebelled," she said, laughing wryly.

Something in Anthony's chest ceased, and it took him a moment to find his words. "I'm sorry you had to go through that."

Gwen shrugged. "It kickstarted the family's first stint at therapy, at least."

Anthony wanted to say more. He hated seeing Gwen unhappy, and watching her on the other side of the couch with her features downturned, all he wanted to do was pull her into his arms.

He wanted to tell her that she deserved someone who'd make her feel safe and a relationship where strife wasn't inevitable. But even in his head, it sounded saccharine, so he let the moment pass without a word.

Chapter Fifteen

GWEN WAS in her classroom with Raven during the lunch period, putting the finishing touches on her room for the school open house in the evening.

Her friend was prattling on about a dress she'd been thinking about buying when she suddenly stopped and asked, "Okay, what's going on, girl? That's like the eighth sigh in two minutes."

Gwen turned to Raven. She thought she'd been hiding her angst well, but evidently not.

"I messed up," Gwen finally said, abandoning the poster board she'd been trying to hang up on the wall with a student's analysis of *A Tale of Two Cities*.

"How badly? Don't tell me you're pregnant," Raven said, hopping off the table she'd been sitting on top of.

"No! If I were, my birth control pills would have a lot of explaining to do."

"Okay," Raven said slowly. "Then what?"

"I got an email from the matchmakers."

"What did it say?"

"I don't know, but it can't be good. I've been a horrible

client recently. I've canceled dates, I've forgotten to finish surveys, and I'm mediocre company when I *do* go out."

"You think they'll be pissed at you for that?"

"Yeah, and also kick me out of the program," Gwen said, dramatically flopping her head backwards.

"But you paid for the service."

"They pride themselves on having a high-quality roster, and my contract has a stipulation that gives them the right to revoke membership for a whole bunch of different reasons."

Gwen hadn't started this matchmaking endeavor just to leave with some nice memories and a smaller bank account.

"Okay, but they could also just be asking you to write a testimonial or give your recommendations for the best sushi restaurants," Raven said. "Show me the email."

She handed her phone over to Raven, and her friend read the message from Hearts Collide as Gwen drummed a rapid beat against her leg.

"Good news or bad news first?" Raven asked after some time.

"Bad. Just get it over with."

"Okay, your phone's software needs to be updated," her friend said. "But the good news is your matchmaker wants to meet with you on Saturday, and there's no indication that you're being fired as a client or anything."

Gwen read the succinct but vague email for herself to confirm.

"What happened, anyway?" Raven asked. "You were so focused and motivated at the beginning."

"Tony happened, and I made it worse by taking your advice."

Her friend's face brightened. "You took my advice? Like, the sex juice cleanse advice?"

"Don't ever use that phrase again, but yeah, that one, and it didn't work."

"Damn. It was that good?"

"Better," Gwen said, slumping into her seat at the front of the classroom.

"Okay. All right. Well, does that have to be a bad thing?" Raven asked. "If I'm being honest, I like Tony for you."

Gwen's head jerked back at Raven's words. She'd have been less thrown if all the inanimate objects in the room had started speaking.

"W-what?" Gwen asked, stunned. "You don't even know him."

"I've met him," Raven said.

"Yeah. Once. For like thirty minutes."

"And what a fantastic first impression. I watched him put his body in harm's way to save children."

"We wouldn't work," Gwen said, a bit disturbed that even her best friend was trying to undermine her efforts.

"Why not?" Raven asked.

"We don't have the same interest or hobbies and—"

"But that's why you have friends. Like he doesn't need to like thrift shopping because, hello! I do. I'll be there."

"He's too grumpy," Gwen said even though she knew it wasn't an accurate assessment.

"From what I saw, he's more of the strong, silent type."

"I don't think he owns pants that aren't made of athletic fabrics."

Her friend put her hands on her hips. "Now, girl… "

"Okay, Raven, what're you doing?"

"I'm trying to be your matchmaker for free. You know, since you think you're about to get sacked."

"I've only really known him for a few weeks."

"So?"

"So, there're bound to be things that come up that make him unsuitable. I don't want to get distracted by superficial stuff."

"I think great sex and intense attraction are important."

Gwen would be lying if she said she didn't feel the pull to throw caution to the wind and follow her heart. But she couldn't. She wasn't like Raven who jumped headfirst into bizarre, wacky, and downright sketchy situations based on a hunch and a whim. To Gwen, that was just a sure way to regret something.

Besides, she'd already invested so much with Hearts Collide. Not just money, but time. And Gwen was unwilling to give up the security, the assurance that they were offering with their system of compatibility.

"I'm just going to stick to what I've been doing," Gwen said.

Raven sighed and said, "Then I guess you'll have to be a big girl and reply to your actual matchmaker."

"I guess so."

———

Anthony ended all his boxing classes the same way, by bowing over his clasped hands and saying, "Hope you got out of this workout what you intended."

Clients would then clean their equipment and head for the door. Only a handful of them would ever linger to ask him a boxing-related question or two.

But something had shifted since he'd appeared on *Cup of Joe* two days ago.

Today, Anthony had barely gotten out his closing sentence after a plyometric-intense class when at least half of the people in the room raced toward him.

"Can I get a picture?" a woman asked.

Someone else hoisted their phone in the air and asked, "Me too?"

"Sure," Anthony replied, quickly wiping the sweat on his face with the front of his t-shirt.

"We saw you on TV," a man wearing a Spotlight-branded shirt said. "Was trying to tell my coworker I knew you."

For several minutes he took selfies and said "Pumpkin" on the count of three and answered the questions about the Giant Pumpkin Rescue, as people had dubbed it.

At the height of his pro boxing career, he'd never really been known outside the boxing world. Fame was for the people who earned millions a match and had sponsorship deals with athleticwear companies.

And the discomfort he felt with all this virality, albeit tame and mostly contained to his city, made him grateful he'd never become a household name back in the day.

By the time Anthony emerged from the downstairs gym, he was exhausted. When he heard someone in the front lobby say his name, he turned on his heel and headed toward the staff room; he needed a break from the fawning.

"Hey, speak of the devil," Lexi, one of the two trainers in the staff room, said when Anthony entered.

"How's it going?" Anthony asked, not even a little curious in what capacity he'd been the subject of conversation. His team seemed to be as enamored by his heroism as the public.

"Have you seen this?" Lexi asked as they stood up and approached Anthony with their phone open to a video.

Someone had taken the part from the original clip of the Giant Pumpkin Rescue where the pumpkin crashed into the wall and added the Kool-Aid Man's "Oh, yeah!"

"Funny," Anthony said, mildly amused, but the two trainers cracked up like it was comedy gold. Lexi slapped their knee while Joshua doubled over, clutching the edge of the table.

Anthony was saved from having to muster up fake laughter when Duncan entered the room.

"There you are," his friend said before walking right up to Anthony and planting a kiss on his sweaty forehead.

"Hi?" Anthony said. "What was that for?"

"I just found out membership applications are up fifteen percent," Duncan said. "And it's all because of you."

"Fifteen?" Anthony asked, his eyes widening.

"Yup, and that's on top of the social media followers we've gained since yesterday and the website traffic that's tripled."

They'd been battling lackluster numbers in their business for months, so this type of growth was worth grinning about.

"This is cause for celebration," Duncan said, pulling out mugs for everyone in the room before cracking open a bottle of kombucha. "Pretend it's champagne."

Once each cup was filled, Duncan raised his mug and said, "To Anthony's thick skull and cat-like reflexes."

———

Stepping into the sterile-looking offices of Hearts Collide Matchmaking felt different for Gwen the second time around. Gone were the excited butterflies in her stomach. All she could feel now was dread.

Sara, the receptionist, greeted her with the same enthusiasm she had the first time and led her to a glass office where Gwen nervously chugged the complimentary water.

After minutes of waiting, she wondered if they were torturing her on purpose.

But just as she'd decided to use the restroom, the door opened. She turned, expecting to see Mary, but a tall blonde woman entered instead. Four people Gwen didn't recognize followed behind, with Mary rounding out the procession.

They really brought in the entire floor when they wanted to dole out bad news. The group, all dressed in white, piled behind the desk with unreadable expressions. Except for Mary, of course, but her smile didn't allay Gwen's nerves.

"I'm Cassidy, the CEO of the Hearts Collide," the blonde woman said, her arms sweeping wide as if she was addressing a crowd instead of just Gwen.

"Nice to meet you," Gwen said, taking a moment to meet everyone's gaze.

"Well, you're probably wondering why we called you in today," Cassidy said as she elbowed for more room. "And it's because something quite unprecedented has happened."

Gwen nodded, taking a deep breath. Not only had she messed things up, but she'd done it royally. An overachiever who even succeeded in failure.

"While you've been with us, you've matched with people with various compatibility percentages. The highest one was seventy-one," Cassidy said. "But I'm pleased to tell you, we've found a match for you who's *ninety-six percent* compatible!"

All at once, everyone in the room started clapping and cheering, and a streamer popper went off, spewing gold confetti into the air.

"N-Ninety-six?" Gwen asked, a bit dazed as someone placed a glass flute in her hand.

"Ninety-six!" Mary shouted as the clapping continued.

The number seemed fake.

"Holy crap," Gwen whispered, taking a swig of her sparkling wine.

She couldn't even begin to imagine the type of man that would fit into that sort of package. Was he somehow her clone? Would they finish each other's sentences and have the same taste in music? God, what if they looked eerily alike?

She took another swig.

"We're in the process of planning an incredibly extravagant first date for you two," a muscular man in a tight blazer said. "Think helicopter ride, a private dinner, and a professional photographer."

"I-I thought date-planning was a gold package perk," Gwen said.

"Well, we thought it was an appropriate exception because your high-level match is a first for the company," Cassidy said. "And, of course, this will be at no additional cost to you so long as we can use your story for promotional purposes."

"Wow, okay. Great. Thank you," Gwen said, still trying to wrap her head around all these developments.

A woman wearing a blouse with poufy sleeves stepped forward and said, "You'll also have access to an award-winning stylist to develop the different looks for your epic date."

"A stylist?" Gwen whispered in disbelief. How many outfits could one person wear on a single date?

"We'll email you in the upcoming days to iron out all the details," Mary said, moving to refill Gwen's glass.

"I don't know what to say," Gwen said.

She suspected she was just feeling overwhelmed by all

the hoopla in the room, and the fact "Here Comes the Bride" was playing off-key in her head.

But she knew the excitement would come once she was able to sit with herself and appreciate how unbelievably lucky she was. This is what she wanted. What she'd been going on date after date for. There was a good chance that Mr. 96% was The One. She was sure the matchmakers in the room were already anticipating all the ways they could blast the successful match on social media.

Cassidy lifted her glass and said, "A toast! To a near-perfect match."

Gwen smiled as she clinked her glass with others in the room, but she forced herself to breathe slowly so as not to empty the contents of her stomach on the lovely carpet.

Chapter Sixteen

DURING THE LAST SCHOOL YEAR, Gwen had come down with a nasty cold that had her in bed for several days. A colleague, a drama teacher named Samantha, had offered to cover her recess supervision duties for the whole week. Grateful, Gwen had told Samantha at the time to hit her up whenever she needed a favor.

That's how Gwen now found herself on a weeknight with the task of carving small to medium pumpkins into jack-o'-lanterns.

Once she accepted she would spend a couple of hours covered in sinewy vegetable mush, Gwen put on a playlist, set up her working space on the kitchen floor, and got down to business.

The first one she did was fun, albeit imperfect. However, Gwen quickly realized she'd overestimated both her carving skills and her wrist strength, and in an hour and a half, she'd made pitiful headway and had almost lost a finger.

Tony arrived home as she was seriously rethinking her

strategy. When he spotted her on the tile floor, surrounded by pumpkins in different stages of mutilation, he paused.

"I think I already had this bad dream," he said.

"Well, it's mine now. I'm doing a colleague a favor, and I thought I'd be done before you got home."

"Do you need help?" he asked.

"You don't have to," she said, eying the pumpkins she had yet to do. "I don't want you traumatized by any more pumpkins."

But he dropped his bags and settled on the other side of the kitchen on the newspaper-covered floor. "It might be therapeutic."

"I'm not going to reject help twice," she said as she passed him a knife and a carving template.

Before she could give him any middling advice, he rolled up his sleeves and attacked the pumpkin with skill and familiarity. For a moment, she was mesmerized by his assured movements. The long muscles in his forearms flexed as he cut a hole out of the top of the pumpkin and roughly pulled out the guts and threw them into the trash can she'd set off to the side.

She took note of the angle of his knife and mimicked it, and it turned out to be the key to easier, smoother carving.

"Dinosaurs, alien invasion, or zombie attack?" Tony asked over the playing music.

"Huh?"

A whisper of a smile tugged at his lips. "It was something the team was arguing about today at the gym. What kind of apocalyptic event would you rather face?"

"Interesting," Gwen said as she thought for a moment. "Which would you prefer?"

"Aliens. They could potentially be reasoned with," he said.

"I think I'd have the best chance of survival with zombies."

"Zombies? Flesh-eating, mindlessly destructive zombies?"

Gwen shrugged. "I feel I can outsmart them."

"So if one burst through that wall right now, what would you do?"

"How much detail do you want?" she asked.

"Moderate."

"Well, I'd first get things to protect myself," Gwen said as she stood up and walked over to a cupboard where she removed a baking sheet.

She then went to the coat closet and pulled out her puffiest jacket and put it on, and as she reentered the kitchen she drew the biggest knife from her knife block.

"Here you go," she said, striking a pose. "Of course, then I'd have to barricade myself in the bathroom till they left.

"Of course," Tony said, nodding seriously but his soft smile grew as he studied her. "What's the coat for?"

"Protection of vital areas, but I'd have to steal a helmet from one of my neighbors."

"You've really thought this through," he said.

"After four hundred seasons of *The Walking Dead*, I'd hope I picked up something," Gwen said as she returned her zombie apocalypse equipment.

They resumed the work at hand and got into a rhythm. The next time they stopped it was because Tony contested the words Gwen was half-singing to an ABBA song.

"Those are not the lyrics," he said.

"Yes, they are," she replied. If there was one thing she knew, it was her beloved Swedish pop group's songs. They were seared into her brain from the countless Saturdays growing up when her mom would blast their greatest hits album as they cleaned the house.

But, to her annoyance and Tony's smugness, she was proven incorrect when he pulled up the lyrics on his phone.

When on her fifth pumpkin of the evening, she explained to Tony a fundamental truth about her job.

"I think if you're going to be a schoolteacher, you have to be prepared to be very uncool at times," she said as Tony chuckled. "It's true! Slang I learn in first period will be outdated by fourth period."

While they swapped out the soggy newspaper they'd been working on, they somehow started discussing their childhood favorite foods, and Tony decided to besmirch the legendary frozen drink that was the Slurpee.

"Weird radioactive sludge," he called them.

"Your point is moot since you just admitted you've never had one," Gwen hotly replied.

"I don't need to touch fire to know it'll hurt me."

As they neared the end, Gwen started teasing Tony about the way he stuck out his tongue a little bit every time he carved a tricky section of the jack-o'-lantern.

"I'm kidding! I'm kidding," she shouted with a laugh as he tossed a handful of pumpkin innards at her.

And when they finally finished carving and clearing the mess they'd made, two hours had passed.

It didn't feel nearly that long.

She'd had fun, and she could admit that she usually enjoyed herself when he was around. Maybe friendship was where they'd land next.

Sure, she was attracted to him to an absurd degree, but that would definitely fade away or become inconsequential. Especially once he moved out and she was officially in a relationship with a suitable guy.

The anxiety at discovering she had a near-perfect match had eased in the proceeding days. And she could even honestly say she felt slight goose bumps when thinking of the upcoming date.

The matchmakers had refused to give her any information on the guy, but that hadn't stopped her from imagining different possible versions of her 96% match in her head. One was arrogant and chatty. Another flirty and eccentric. And her favorite one was nerdy and sophisticated.

After slipping into her room to change into clothes not covered in pumpkin, Gwen returned to the kitchen where Tony was eating leftovers from a bowl and scrolling through his phone.

Strong and thoughtful.

Gwen shook her head the moment the thought surfaced. Tony wasn't some potential romantic candidate.

Friends.

She could do that.

———

When Anthony arrived home, he'd intended to have a chill evening and decompress from another long day at work and the seemingly never waning fanfare. An evening of carving pumpkins was not what he had in mind, but somehow it had been exactly what he needed.

Being around Gwen nourished a side of him that often got neglected.

He was polishing off his dinner when Gwen reemerged from her bedroom wearing a different sweater and pair of jeans.

"There's still some rice in the fridge if you want some," he said.

"Oh, I already ate," she said. "But I am craving a Slurpee, so I think I'm going to go get one."

"Right now?" he asked, looking at the time on his phone.

"Slurpees and cereal are two things that you can have at any point in the day," she said as she pulled her coat from the closet and shrugged it on. "Do you wanna come? Maybe get one for yourself?"

"Not even a little."

"Oh, come on," she said, approaching him and wrapping her hands around his forearms. "It'll give you a chance to make an informed opinion."

It was dark and frigid outside. No place he'd like to be, but he wanted to extend their evening together. She was also touching him, sending little sparks up and down his arm, so he said, "Fine, let's go."

They decided to walk the few blocks to the store, and as they made their way out of the building and through the parking area onto the sidewalk, Gwen asked, "How exactly does one get to be as old as you are and never try a Slurpee?"

"Besides the radioactive sludge thing?"

"Yes, besides that," she said, laughing.

"My parents didn't allow sugar in the house growing up," he said.

Of course, he eventually had the opportunity when he got into grade school to eat anything he wanted while out with friends, but he'd never had a sweet tooth, preferring to go for the corn dogs and nachos slathered in fake cheese.

"Do they live here?" Gwen asked. "Your parents?"

"No, they live in Hamilton now," he said.

"But I'm sure they've heard all about the local clout you've accrued?" she said, wiggling her eyebrows.

Anthony laughed a little bit. "No, but we don't talk much, so maybe they do know."

"Oh," Gwen said, her smile dimming.

Anthony hadn't meant to bring the mood down and quickly said, "We're not estranged or anything, just not close."

She looked at him and nodded. "I get that."

Perhaps it was the open and non-pressuring silence Gwen let hang between them that made him want to say more.

"They're serious people," he said when they came to a red light at an intersection. "Not the affectionate type. I don't think my dad has ever told me he loves me."

It was a realization that he'd come to as an adult, and he'd never shared it with anyone. It was not exactly something you slip into a conversation.

"I'm sorry," Gwen said softly, looping her arm through his.

The unexpected gesture brought on a sudden tightness in his chest.

"It's okay," he said, but maybe some Rorschach inkblot test would say otherwise.

Regardless, he'd somehow been able to cultivate a life where he was surrounded by people who for some reason or another wanted him there. Duncan, his team at Spotlight, and of course, Old Man Enoch and Ms. Katherine.

They finished their short journey in comfortable silence, their condensed breaths swirling in puffs in front of them. When they entered the harshly lit store, Gwen pointed to the Slurpee machine and said, "There she is."

He looked at the brightly multi-colored slush churn, unable to understand the appeal.

Gwen strode to the station and handed him a cup. "My favorite flavors are blue raspberry and pina colada."

"I'mma go with orange," he said, pulling the lever to release the slop into his cup.

"How pedestrian," Gwen said as she created her concoction.

When they got to the checkout, Gwen insisted on paying for his drink saying, "My thanks for helping me with the carving."

Once outside, they both took their first sip.

"Ah," Gwen shouted into the open sky. "That's good stuff right there."

Anthony kept on taking tentative drinks, waiting for the "good" to kick in.

"What do you think?" she asked him.

"Tastes like a heartburn waiting to happen," he said.

She laughed. "You gotta try at least two other flavors before you make your final verdict."

There was no way he was ever trying one again; in fact, he regretted not tossing the one he held before they'd started their trek back home. His fingers were turning numb from the cold.

"How are you just holding this?" he asked, looking at her as she held the frozen beverage in her bare hand and didn't seem at all bothered.

"Practice," she said.

He was almost positive this was the process of cryonics because surely his organs were dissipating and his brain function slowing. But he gritted his teeth and ignored the voice telling him to toss the cup onto the sidewalk.

When they finally got back to the apartment, he immediately abandoned the cup and headed to the sink to run his hands under warm water.

Meanwhile, Gwen leaned over the counter and continued to enjoy her drink as she watched Anthony try to revive the feeling in his fingers.

"Any nerve damage?" Gwen asked.

He turned around to answer seriously, but then he caught the teasing curve of her smile.

"You think my pain is a joke?" he asked, stalking toward her but unable to fully suppress the smile on his own face.

"No, I think it's cute."

"I don't think anyone has ever called me cute," he said.

She raised her hands. "Oh, my apologies. I didn't mean to threaten your boxer persona."

"Now what's my boxer persona?" he asked.

"You know, tough guy. Doesn't take shit," she said, turning her lips down and putting on an aggressive scowl.

"Is that supposed to be my face?" he asked.

"Yes," she said, exaggerating her expression even more.

"I had no idea I looked like a troll under a bridge," he said.

"Sure, if trolls were mysterious and sexy."

The word "sexy" dropped from her mouth, ricocheted off the walls, traveled through space and time before breaking the sound barrier.

He knew she hadn't meant to say all that from the widening of her eyes, but it was too late. And somewhere between an exhale and a blink of an eye, their bodies met in a fury of heat and anticipation.

Chapter Seventeen

"MY BED," she said against his lips as he half carried her through the apartment.

Dumping her on her bed, she lay sprawled on her back looking at him. The light from above cast a hypnotic gleam to her eyes.

"You're incredible," she whispered as her gaze roamed his body and face.

Something in his chest jumped at her assertion. She looked at him as if he were some pretty painting strung up in a museum, and he was just far gone enough in his lust to believe it.

Sitting up, she pulled his shirt over his head, and he returned the favor by removing her sweater and unhooking her bra.

Her nipples, a few shades darker than her brown skin, were hardened to the most delectable points already. He captured one of her nipples in his mouth while he agitated the other with his fingers, pleased when her breathing quickly turned shallow.

Her hands found the back of his head, and she brought their lips together and fell back onto the mattress.

With every swipe of her tongue and gentle moan, he sunk deeper into the intoxicating embrace of his desire for her. He needed to get her completely naked.

Reaching for the waist of her jeans, he pulled them down her soft thighs, relishing the way she gripped his shoulders as he did so.

Once she was clad in just her sheer lacy underwear, he lowered himself onto his knees between her thighs. His chest barely contained his racing heart as she spread her legs wider to accommodate his broad body.

He draped either of her legs over his shoulders, loving the weight of them. Anchoring him to this moment.

"I can't wait to taste you again," he said, feeling the responding goose bumps on her calves.

He worked his way along her inner thighs, kisses and licking her warm skin. She squirmed under his touch as if urging him to hurry up. But he needed to go slow. He wanted her to come in a way that would rip the fabric of space and time.

When he reached her already wet panties, he gently stroked her clit with his thumb. Each brush drew out the sweetest whimpers from her.

"That feel good?" he asked, sounding raspy.

"Tony, please," she whispered.

Hearing the need in her voice, brazen and desperate, had him abandoning his promise to take things at a steady pace, and he peeled her underwear off in one fluid motion. Her slick, slightly swollen folds greeted him on the other side.

"Jesus, baby," he said before he descended on her pussy with a sort of reverence. He watched her intently as he flattened his tongue against her core and dragged it all the way up to her sensitive bud.

The sigh that fell from her lips had his dick pressing hard against the front of his pants, and he continued taking laps up and down her sweet pussy. He soon adjusted his pressure and zeroed in on her clit, and it wasn't long before her ass came off the bed and her legs bore down on his shoulders.

Her enthusiasm and her desire hit him like a wave. He pulled her closer to his mouth, wanting her to take every iota of pleasure he could muster from her.

"That fucking tongue," she said. "I fucking love…"

Her breath hitched as he slipped his middle finger into her pussy and began pumping. She was so wet, so hungry. And it was the way she held on to her own breasts and pinched her nipples that had him fisting his hard length.

One of her hands settled on the back of his head, and when she tightened her grip on his curls, he released a deep moan that had her writhing against his face.

"Yeah, just like that. Yes," she said between gasps, her eyes rolling back a bit.

Gwen. His beautiful Gwen on the verge of climax. He slipped in another finger, knowing how much she loved it. She bucked against his face as he fucked her pussy, and she didn't stop until she was whimpering his name on the tail end of a moan.

———

This was the last time.

It had to be.

But as Tony's body hovered over her, his dick poised to enter her, she couldn't remember why she thought platonic friendship was a good idea. She couldn't stop looking at his face, so serious and attentive. Like he took her pleasure as thoughtfully as anything important in his life.

He lowered his lips, kissing her deeply as his dick slowly sank into her pussy.

She gasped into his mouth, feeling the glorious fullness and friction build as he continued to retreat and surge into her. The power behind each thrust raised goose bumps on her skin.

When he looked between their bodies and then back at her, her breath caught in her throat. How was she going to make do without this?

"I want you to play with that pretty clit for me," he said, kissing the side of her mouth.

As she did as he instructed, it seemed all the nerves on the surface of her body were firing off, leaving her barely able to draw a breath. She pressed her face into the crook of Tony's neck and muttered words she wasn't sure made any sense.

"This what you need?" he asked, his hands gripping her hips in an almost-painful hold.

"Harder," she whispered as if she weren't already coming undone.

Suddenly, he stopped and pulled himself out of her. It happened so quickly she was gasping at the loss.

"Tony," she said as she grabbed for his shoulders to pull him back on top of her.

But he had other things in mind because he flipped her over onto her hands and knees and positioned them to face the mirror above her dresser. Her eyes were heavy with lust and lips parted on uneven breaths.

"You ready, beautiful?" he asked her, meeting her eye.

The way he said it. The way he was watching her. It sent tingles all across her body.

"Fuck me," she said before he eased himself into her again.

In this position, she could see the sweat on his brown skin and the muscles in his torso and arms ripple as he held her about her waist.

"Such a perfect pussy," he said, bringing her up and down his length with increasing force.

Watching him so focused, his eyebrows drawn and his lips in a firm line, and knowing it was all in service of fucking her had her clit pulsing.

There came a moment where she couldn't hold herself up anymore and she thought she would collapse, but Tony wrapped his arm around her waist and flattened her back against his chest and buried his face into her short coils.

She held onto his forearm as his pace increased. His warm breath tickled her neck, and with each thrust, she was shoved closer and closer to her end.

"Who gets this pussy wet, baby?" he asked against her ear.

Her heart was drumming aggressively against her chest and her vision was blurry as she cried out, "You do!"

Had she ever felt this way? Completely and totally absorbed in the moment. This man, an addictive mix of stern and tender, was doing things to her that she wouldn't be able to understand for a while.

Because when he said in a deep gruff voice, "My motherfucking pussy," as he continued to drive his dick into her, the unexpected possessiveness didn't throw her off at all. Instead of the awkwardness she might've felt if it were anyone else, hearing him say those words was so fucking hot that it edged her to the precipice of her orgasm. All it took was a few more pumps, and she was screaming his name and digging her nails into his arms.

They lay there in post-sex bliss. He wanted to trap this moment and live in it on an endless loop. The feeling of her soft limbs against him, the gentle scent of her skin, the way she caressed his chest.

Words he'd not intended to say had slipped out while they fucked. He'd been too possessive. But her response had been positive, enthusiastic even. It had dragged all his emotions to the surface, and he'd yet to suppress them again.

It felt like he had a stick of dynamite in his chest that could go off at any moment. And as he stared at the ceiling, holding her, a truth swirled around him, one that would not be ignored.

He was in love with Gwen Gilmore.

Anthony was sure it happened long before that moment, and it was almost laughable how he'd tried to delude himself into thinking it was simply attraction. Every time he was around her he felt like gravity might cease to hold him down and he'd float away into the clouds. This beautiful, clever woman with a contagious laugh had his heart, and he didn't know what to do about it.

"You're tense," Gwen whispered, shifting closer to him. "Penny for your thoughts?"

He didn't respond right away, the words clogging his throat. Could he tell her? Put his heart out there without any real plan or sense of where she was at?

"I-I'm… just thinking about the gym," he said, feeling immediately like the biggest coward.

She propped herself on her elbow to look at him. "How's everything going?"

"We've seen an increase in all the important metrics," he said leaving out the fact he was quickly growing sick of recounting the rescue. He felt like a broken record, but it was a small price to pay for business growth.

"That's fantastic," she said, beaming at him. "Very happy for you."

That dimpled smile of hers that pressed her full lips upward had him almost blurting out everything on his mind and heart. She might not be in love with him, but it was reasonable for him to assume that she at least liked spending time with him and sharing her bed. Something more could develop. Maybe he could ask her out on a date. Do the whole wooing thing. He had no idea how to do it, but he was sure the internet was chock full of advice.

While a plan started forming in his head, Gwen lightly slapped him on the chest and said, "Oh, I also have some good, sorta weird news, courtesy of my matchmaker."

Anthony's stomach dropped, and a high-pitched sound started ringing in his ears as she began to speak.

He didn't pick up all the words she said, but he got the gist.

"Ninety-six," he finally said after taking several moments. The number felt like poison on his tongue.

"I know. It sounds unreal. My perfect match. Or rather my *near*-perfect match," she said with an airy laugh.

"T-that's… good," he said as a numbness settled into his body.

"They're planning this whole dramatic super date for us, to optimize the falling-in-love potential, I guess."

Each sentence was worse than the next, and it was a wonder Anthony was still able to draw breath.

Ninety-six.

Ninety-fucking-six.

This is what she'd been looking for. How could he compete with statistical perfection? Part of him, the part that was adaptable and didn't give a damn about the odds stacked against him, wanted to tell her to forget whatever guy the matchmakers thought was best for her and choose him instead. But he didn't move. And as the minutes stretched and his mind continued to reel, Gwen's body relaxed and her breathing grew even.

It took him a while longer to fall asleep, and he expected his sleep to be restless and tormented, but it was the exact opposite.

He had a wonderful dream that *he* was Gwen's 96% compatible guy. They were both elated about the discovery and proceeded to frolic through a random lavender field, laughing and humming songs neither knew the lyrics to.

And because of the weird nature of dreams, they somehow ended up stumbling across a water fountain in the middle of the field.

"Let's swim," Dream Gwen said, as she dropped the sundress she wore to expose her incredible body.

He smiled, reaching out for her, but before he could touch her, he was lurched out of the fantasy.

Anthony's eyes fluttered open as he oriented himself.

It was morning, and he was still in Gwen's room.

His mind was still hazy and operating under a film. So when the woman of his literal dreams suddenly appeared in the doorway of her bedroom wearing a nice dark green dress that complimented her skin tone and wielding a tube of lipstick, it felt like a continuation of his fantasy.

"You working late today?" Gwen asked. "I was thinking of Thai for dinner. I can grab you some if you want."

"Thai sounds good," he said, his voice scratchy.

She flashed him a smile before retreating. And as he swung his legs out of bed and sat on the edge, he felt a glow radiating from the surface of his body.

But he was quickly and effortlessly brought back to reality by an incoming text that lit up his phone's screen:

Dear resident of Clover Apartment Complex. We're delighted to inform you that your apartment will be ready for you to move back into by the end of the workweek. We hope the delay wasn't too much of an inconvenience, and we thank you for your patience.

———

Gwen tried not to fidget as she watched the buttons of the elevator light up on her ascent to her apartment floor. Today had been relatively dull at work, but she couldn't wait to see Tony and tell him all about it.

It had been a couple of days since they'd last slept together, and she'd barely seen him except for the quick moments in the morning. But it was the weekend, and she didn't have a date lined up until Mr. 96%, so she thought she'd suggest they go to the night market near her place.

This was her first step in putting Tony in the platonic metaphorical box he belonged in. Sure, she'd caught herself a couple times throughout the day thinking about how his body felt on hers or the specific timbre of his voice, but what counted was she was trying.

The door of the elevator opened, and she forced herself to take dignified steps toward her apartment instead of the hasty ones she wanted. Upon entering her home, however, all her bright energy left her with stunning swiftness when she spotted Tony's suitcase and duffle bag sitting packed near the entrance.

"Hey," Tony said, appearing from the bathroom, holding some of his toiletries.

"You're leaving," she said, dragging her eyes from his luggage to look at him. She was proud her voice sounded even and strong.

Tony paused for a moment before saying, "Yeah, my apartment's livable again."

"That's great," she said, forcing herself to smile. Of course this was a good thing. They'd been working toward this nebulous move-out date. And the time had come. She'd finally get her space back, and the waters of whatever was going on between them could clear.

"Those are for you," Tony said, pointing to a grand bouquet of white and pale pink flowers that sat on top of her counter in a vase that she only now noticed.

God knew how she'd missed them when she'd walked in. They certainly were the most extravagant arrangement she'd ever received. She approached them now and lightly ran her fingers over the velvety petals and lush leaves.

"They're beautiful," she said softly before picking up the card.

"Thank you," it simply read.

She looked over at him. "You really should learn how to be more succinct."

He offered her one of his infrequent small smiles and said, "I do appreciate it, and I'm sorry I've been in your way."

"No, not at all. It's been good."

More than good. But she didn't say that.

They both regarded each other for a moment before Gwen extended her hand out in front of her for a handshake. She didn't know why she did it, but he didn't even hesitate before taking her hand in his to complete the gesture.

"Stay"—she coughed as the words caught in her throat —"in touch."

He responded with a nod before picking up his bags and heading toward the door.

"Bye, Gwen."

Just like that.

She was left staring at the door he shut behind himself for several seconds before turning to face the interior of her apartment. The appliances and furniture were all how she'd set them up, but it seemed empty. A weird and unexplainable feeling took root in her chest. One she refused to interrogate at that moment.

Chapter Eighteen

WHEN ENOCH and Ms. Katherine's front door opened, Anthony expected to be greeted like he typically was when he visited, with casual hugs and inquiries about his week.

Instead, he'd barely stepped inside the home when the older couple began goofing around.

"Look, there he is!" Ms. Katherine said, making camera-flashing sounds.

Enoch crowded him and held up an invisible camera and shouted, "Anthony Woods! Anthony Woods! Over here!"

"Do you think fame has changed you?" Ms. Katherine asked. "If so, how?"

"Okay, all right," Anthony said, unable to stop the smile on his face.

It felt like it had been several lifetimes since the Great Pumpkin Rescue, but in fact, it had only been two weeks.

"Your picture is up on the Fall Harvest Festival website," Enoch said, taking Anthony's coat from him.

"At this point, I think that's the least weird thing to come out of the whole thing," he said.

"I'm so proud of you," Ms. Katherine said.

Enoch nodded and declared, "All's well that ends well."

Anthony entered the home fully, immediately spotting the lamps and side table meant for him. Now that he was finally back in his apartment, he was picking up the furniture he'd been scheduled to get over a month ago.

"I know you can't stay long, but we were just making some hot chocolate with Enoch's homemade marshmallows," Ms. Katherine said.

"I have time for a mug," he said, moving into the kitchen.

As the couple finished prepping the hot drinks, Anthony went to study the odd objects occupying the surface of the breakfast nook. There was a magnifying glass desk lamp, paint tubes, and several odd-shaped metal tools.

"What's the project?" Anthony asked Enoch.

"Miniature clay art," the old man said, coming over to hold up some of his creations.

"An owl?" Anthony asked, pointing at the brown blob.

Enoch grinned. "Exactly right."

"Here we go," Ms. Katherine said, approaching with full mugs.

Anthony relieved her of the tray and found a spot for it on the busy table.

With them all seated, Anthony fished out a floating marshmallow from his cup and popped it into his mouth. "It's good."

"I tweaked the recipe a little," Enoch explained. "You should take some for Gwen. I'm sure she'd enjoy them."

Anthony nodded without commitment. Since moving out of her apartment, he'd been walking a tightrope in regards to thinking about Gwen. Most times he could convince himself that his feelings for her were inconsequential to him, like jewelry trends and the state of Greenland's soccer team. Like maybe he'd somehow hoodwinked himself into believing he was in love with her because he enjoyed being in her company and the sex was fantastic.

But every so often he'd look down from his high-wire act and freak out. Just yesterday morning, he was in his kitchen pouring himself a glass of orange juice when he'd thought he better leave enough for Gwen. The instinctive thought had left him in a daze for a few minutes.

He was grateful that work had been busy recently. It afforded the distraction he desperately needed. There was barely enough time to replenish his electrolytes, never mind think about his emotional state.

"How is Gwen?" Ms. Katherine asked.

"Fine," Anthony replied, trying to keep his voice even. "You do know I've moved out of her apartment, right?"

"Yes, but…" Enoch said as he exchanged a look with his wife. "We thought you…" The old man hemmed and hawed for a moment.

"What?" Anthony asked.

"We thought there was something going on between you and Gwen," Ms. Katherine finally said.

"No, nothing," he replied.

"But soon, right?" Ms. Katherine asked. "Like those beginning stages where you haven't defined the relationship?"

"Gwen and I are not together and never will be," he said.

"Oh. I guess we misread that situation," Enoch said.

"Can you blame us? There was only one bedroom in her apartment," Ms. Katherine said.

"There was a pull-out couch."

"Well, there were also the eyes you were making at each other," Enoch said.

"Eyes?" Anthony asked.

"Yeah, like—" Enoch squinted and ducked his head in a coy way.

"Nobody did that," Anthony said, mortified at the idea of being so transparent.

The old man patted him on the back. "We've established that we misread things."

The trio moved onto different, less awkward subjects, and even played a card game before Anthony left. When he arrived home and entered his apartment, the rattling of the recently reinvigorated heating system welcomed him.

He placed his newly acquired furniture down and turned on the TV to stave off unwanted thoughts. But as he washed the dishes he'd let accumulate the last few days, an emptiness, vast and gnawing, surfaced.

Fuck.

He leaned over the sink and closed his eyes.

It had been a week; there should have been some respite from these feelings by now. Instead, his home, a place he'd lived in longer than any other place as an adult, felt foreign to him. And he was a prisoner in his own mind.

But maybe he was going about getting over Gwen in the wrong way.

In the pro-boxing world, he'd been known as an out-fighter, someone who preferred to keep space between his opponent and use his long reach. Swarmers, or pressure-fighters, had always been his favorite type of boxers to watch and compete against. Their persistent and aggressive style was fun to witness and always kept him on his toes in the ring.

He'd been waiting to get over Gwen with a passivity that clearly wasn't working. He needed to take a page from the swarmer fight book and expel these feelings with a little more intention and vigor.

Wiping his hands against his pants, Anthony pulled out his phone and scrolled through the trash folder of his email, looking for a discarded correspondence. When he found it, he composed and sent an email before the fury of inspiration could dissipate.

He had to move on, no matter how drastic the measures.

———

"Mom!" Gwen shouted into the quiet house.

She trudged through the kitchen into the living room before peeking through a window into the backyard. No luck.

"Mom!" she shouted again as she headed upstairs.

"You came!" her mom responded finally, popping her head out of the master bedroom.

The older woman was in a fluffy bathrobe, her hair was in rollers, and she wore plum lipstick.

"Yeah, of course I came," Gwen said as she climbed the remaining steps.

Her mom had sent her a cryptic but frantic text to come over. She'd used Gwen's full name and everything.

"You said it was an emergency, and I find you having a spa day—"

Gwen froze when she stepped into her mother's room.

"My God. What's happening here?" Gwen asked, looking around the room where seemingly her mother's entire closet was scattered across the bed and different pairs of shoes acted as tripping hazards on the floor.

"Nothing. It's a little bit of a mess. I'm getting ready for a date," her mother said, walking into the en suite bathroom.

"I'm sorry, did you say a date?" Gwen asked, following her mother.

The bathroom was in similar disarray as the bedroom with various beauty products and cosmetics crowding the counter.

"I did. After the last family brunch, I kept thinking that if your dad is already dating, why can't I?"

"But you're ready for it, right? It's not just a way to show Dad you're over him or something?" Gwen asked as she moved the burning incense stick on the counter to the windowsill.

"Yes, I'm ready. I think I was just scared, and I needed that jolt to get me out there. So I went on Facebook and found someone," her mom said brightly.

"What do you mean, you *found* someone?" Gwen asked. The last thing she needed was her mom in some sticky situation with a scammer or axe murderer.

"Stanley Pale," her mom said in an almost breathy tone. "I knew him in high school and had the biggest crush on him. But like most kids after high school, we went our separate ways."

"He was your high school boyfriend?"

"No, just a boy who was sort of a friend. We had a few classes together. I contacted him through social media, we started talking, and he asked me on a date." Her mom laughed and flung her arms up in an amused shrug.

"That's great," Gwen said, genuinely happy for her mother. "And we can talk about it if you want, but why am I here right now?"

"I need you to drive me there."

"What's wrong with your car or an Uber?" Gwen asked.

"You know I don't like taking Ubers at night. And I can't drive my car because the edible I took is kicking in right about now."

"Jesus, Mom."

"I was anxious. I haven't done this in three decades," her mother said as she turned to the mirror and opened her eyes wide to apply mascara.

"Let me do that before you have to go on your date with an eye patch," Gwen said, taking the mascara wand.

"Any advice?" her mom asked. "What should I expect?"

Gwen shrugged. "It depends on what kind of person you go out with, but all you can do is put the best version of yourself out there and have an exit plan if things go south."

Gwen closed the tube once she was done, and left the bathroom so her mother could finish getting ready. She headed straight to the bed and fell on her back onto the mattress full of clothes.

"Did your brother tell you about the fifteen-percent increase in membership sign-ups since Anthony's TV appearance?" her mother asked from the other room.

"Yeah, he did," Gwen replied, feeling something in her chest shift at the mention of Tony.

For all intents and purposes, Tony had ceased to matter in her life, but she couldn't quit thinking of him. What was even more surprising was the feeling of something close to sadness that sprang up every time she did.

Tony had never been a loud or aggressively present person in her apartment, but it felt oddly quiet and still without him there. And it took several days before she remembered she could move around freely and with as few clothes on as she wanted.

If she were brave enough, she could've just texted him

that she wanted to hang out or something. But the thought of him tepidly replying or agreeing just to be nice was enough for her to drop the idea.

He would just have to be a moment in her life she looked back fondly on. And it wasn't like she'd *never* see him again. He was still her brother's best friend.

"Should I go with the shawl or blazer?" Gwen's mom asked as she emerged from the bathroom holding the two garments.

Gwen looked up. "I like the shawl."

"Perfect. Me too," her mom replied before disappearing once again.

Gwen lay back down as a buzz from her phone alerted her to a new text. She swore under her breath when she saw who the message was from. Her matchmaker and the other professionals who were planning the big extravagant date with Mr. 96%, had been texting and emailing her incessantly all week.

One message might be about her shoe size, and another would ask about her favorite foods. There was so much fuss and excitement over particularities that it quickly got annoying. More than once, Gwen felt tempted to ask if they could just have a date at a mall Starbucks.

Wouldn't that be the test of a real connection anyway, to engage with a person while doing the most mundane things? The memory of eating ice cream with Tony on the couch came to mind.

Her phone buzzed again, and she tossed it over the edge of the bed. "Shut up."

"Baby, what's wrong?" her mom asked.

"Nothing," Gwen said as her mom took a seat beside her on the bed.

"You feeling okay?" the older woman asked, placing a palm on her forehead.

"Never been better. Why do you ask?"

"Come on, love. Talk to me."

Gwen turned to look at her mom and hesitated for a beat. "My matchmakers are pissing me off. They won't stop texting and emailing me."

"Isn't that what you're paying them to do? You have this upcoming date with that perfect match, right?"

"Yeah. It's just everyone is putting a lot of stock and effort into this one date, and I'm worried about potentially not connecting with him," Gwen said, sitting up to look more directly into her mother's face. "What if he thinks I'm over-opinionated or I don't like the way he laughs?"

This matchmaking thing wasn't a hard science, after all. Mr. 96% could just be where all her hopes and dreams went to die. And at that point, where else was there to go? He was near perfect.

"I can't help but feel responsible for this," Gwen's mom said after a sigh.

"What're you talking about?" Gwen asked, frowning. "Why would you feel responsible?"

"All your anxiety and hang-ups about love are because of me and your dad. We weren't exactly the best model of a healthy relationship, and it affected you and Duncan. I'm sorry about that."

Gwen stared at her mother for a long moment, a little taken aback that they were even having this discussion. These types of conversations had always been facilitated by a therapist in the past.

"It's okay, Ma," Gwen said.

"No, it's not, baby. I know you're scared of ending up in a miserable relationship, but I don't want you to sabotage yourself by chasing perfection."

Her mother's words affirmed what Gwen already knew.

She couldn't let the nagging feeling of discontentment dictate her next steps.

"I hear you," she replied, taking her mom's hand.

She simply had to hold onto the hope that her perseverance through the matchmaking process would be rewarded.

Chapter Nineteen

A HEAVY KNOCK sounded at Anthony's door, pulling him out of his nap. He sprang up from his couch and picked up the bowl full of candy on his way to answer it.

"Trick or treat!" two kids shouted once the door had opened.

One was dressed as Captain America and the other as a princess, and they held out their bags as Anthony placed handfuls of candy in each.

"Happy Halloween," he said to them before they raced to the next apartment.

Once he shut the door, he retraced his steps to his couch to wait for the next batch of trick or treaters. The holiday had snuck up on Anthony; he'd only realized it was Halloween when he'd arrived at the gym and felt like he'd stepped into a Party City. After work, he'd scavenged three different stores for enough candy for the children in the apartment complex.

Another knock echoed through the apartment, and he expected to find more kids in costumes based on movies and shows he was unfamiliar with. Instead, it was his best friend dressed as a pirate, eye patch and a fake parrot on his shoulder included.

"How did you get in the building?" Anthony asked.

"You gave me a key, remember?" Duncan said, pushing past him to get inside.

"For emergencies, yes. Why're you here?"

"Because it's Halloween, and we're going to a party," Duncan said as he studied the contents of the candy bowl in Anthony's hand.

"I'm not going anywhere—"

"I was thinking about what you could pull off last minute, and I came up with a WWE wrestler or a cat," Duncan said as he tore into a mini chocolate bar.

"A cat?" Anthony asked.

"You know, a temperamental creature that likes to be left alone. I thought it would be easy for you to get into character. Plus, I have the ears in my truck."

"I'm not going anywhere," Anthony said.

"It'll be fun. Retta's friend, Nia, throws the best parties. Expensive liquor, in-demand DJs."

Duncan had to know that none of the details had any bearing on Anthony's disinterest. In Anthony's estimation, the two worst people to be at a party were the one who refused to actually party and the person who didn't know when to stop taking shots. He was the former.

"Why are you pushing this so hard, man?" Anthony asked.

"Because you need to get out more."

Anthony frowned. "We've been friends for too long for that to suddenly be a problem."

Duncan sighed. "I think something happened to you and your mystery woman, and I don't like seeing my best friend sad, okay?"

"I don't know what you're talking about," Anthony said, avoiding his friend's eye.

"Come on, man. I know something is up," Duncan said. "You signed up to be the bachelor for *I Choose You!* for God's sake."

It was true. The evening after visiting Enoch and Ms. Katherine, Anthony emailed the producer who'd offered him the position as the bachelor for the *I Choose You!* segment on *Cup of Joe Morning Show*.

He'd known it was a long shot that the spot would still be open or that they'd even want him, not only because of his waning relevancy but also because he'd emphatically rejected the position in the first place. But he hadn't even had a chance to regret the email before the producer replied, excited. His ludicrous, desperate plan to get over heartbreak was officially in motion.

"Let's just cut the bullshit," Duncan said.

Anthony rubbed his head. "I fell in love with her, okay? Happy?"

Duncan broke into a wide smile and said, "I knew it. I fucking knew it—"

"Listen, this doesn't have some happily ever after."

"But it could!" Duncan said, bouncing on his toes. "Not so long ago, you told me to go out on a limb and tell Retta my feelings for her, and now I'm telling you the same thing."

"Well, I won't be taking that advice, considering she's in love with someone else."

Or she would be soon enough.

His friend's smile dimmed, and he grew still. "Dammit. I'm sorry, man."

"I'm good," Anthony said, coughing to clear the sudden lump in his throat.

"Then the *I Choose You!* gig is—"

"A misguided attempt to get over her? Yes. But at the very least, we'll get more buzz for the gym."

Duncan stood there silent for a second as if trying to absorb everything he'd just learned before he pulled out his cellphone and asked, "Pepperoni or Hawaiian?"

"What?"

"Pepperoni or Hawaiian?"

"Why—What are you doing?" Anthony asked, watching his friend enter the living room and slump into the couch and kick his feet up.

"Ordering pizza."

"I thought you were going to that party," Anthony said.

"Nah, change of plans," Duncan said, removing his eye patch. "I'm staying in with my lovesick friend and watching bad '80s action movies."

Anthony wanted to reject the offer as unnecessary and restate his emotional stability. But Duncan had already logged into a streaming service on the TV, and Anthony was tired of pretending.

So he sank onto his sofa beside his best friend and said, "Pepperoni."

———

Gwen felt like a lab rat.

For the last hour and a half, she'd been poked and prodded during the makeup trial run for her mega date with Mr. 96%. She had no idea how the look was coming along since she'd been prohibited from seeing herself in the mirror until the look was complete. Instead, she'd been staring at a glass shelf with half a dozen brands of hand lotion.

"Relax your face, hon," the makeup artist, Tori, said.

"Sorry," Gwen replied, trying to still her thoughts so she wouldn't emote.

"No, it's all right. I can imagine you must be just a bundle of nerves and excitement," Tori said as she applied a lipstick called "Rockin' Slappin' Bitchin' Pink" to Gwen's lips.

Gwen had dragged herself out of her emotional funk by adopting an outlook of unbound optimism. Her annoyance with the fuss, she realized, was admitting failure in the middle of a marathon. So for the past couple of days, whenever she received a text or an email from the matchmaking staff, she would grin and smother thoughts that were anything less than positive.

"Almost done, Mary! Then she's all yours," Tori said, turning to the matchmaker who'd been working on her phone on the other side of the small beauty boutique. A garment bag that held the dress Gwen would wear on the evening portion of her date lay across Mary's lap.

With a final brush stroke and a cool spritz of a setting spray, Tori finally backed away from Gwen and assessed her work.

"Are you ready to see how pretty you look?" Tori asked as Mary stood up to join them for the reveal.

Gwen nodded as the makeup artist spun her chair around to face the mirror.

"Ta-da!"

"What the fu—" Gwen cut herself off and clamped her lips tightly.

For many seconds she didn't know what to say. She looked like she'd dunked her face in a basin full of chalky dust found on powdered donuts. All she needed was a red nose and unicycle to complete the look.

"The foundation color's a bit off, no?" Mary asked carefully, studying Gwen in the mirror.

"Yeah, a darker shade would work better," Tori said, twisting her head as if she was only just considering it.

Gwen held herself from saying "No shit" as she took in more details of the ghastly look that the morning sun streaming in from the windows only emphasized.

"I'll get it right on the day," Tori said, nodding seriously. "But everything else is perfect."

"Okay, then let's go try on your dress," Mary said as she practically dragged Gwen to her feet and towards the staff room at the back of the boutique.

"See how that one fits," Mary said as she handed her the garment bag and pushed her behind a dressing screen. "This will be the outfit you'll wear at the evening portion of the date. Which I know you're going to absolutely die over. We're sending you guys to an award-winning steakhouse…"

As Mary prattled on about details of the date, Gwen shimmied her way into the dress. It took a hot minute because she kept catching her ashy reflection in the tiny mirror on the wall and getting distracted.

With the dress finally on, Gwen realized that it was way too tight around her chest, and the straps dug into her shoulders uncomfortably. She also wasn't confident that the bodice would stay intact if she were to bend over.

"Hey, Mary?" Gwen called out. "I think you got the wrong dress size."

"Come on out and let me see."

She rounded the corner and went to stand with Mary in front of a full-length mirror.

The Bride of Frankenstein was all she saw.

"We'll let it out a bit," Mary said breezily like that would fix the absolute travesty that was the fit of the dress.

But instead of complaining or freaking out, Gwen just

smiled and nodded. This experience was a privilege and a delight. And everything was just fine.

"Okay, let's try on the shoes," Mary said as she pulled out a pair of heels from one of the bags she'd been carrying.

The moment the sparkly shoes were in Gwen's hands, she knew they were too big, but she put them on anyway.

When she stood up and walked across the room, the shoes slipped off her heels with every step. The clopping sound they made against the tile reminded Gwen of a galloping horse, and suddenly everything became funny.

A laugh, unbridled and from her gut, erupted from Gwen.

"A-are you okay?" Mary asked softly.

"Look at me," Gwen said as she continued to laugh and prance around the room.

The dress didn't fit, the makeup looked like she was due for a casket, and the shoes made her feel like a child playing dress-up. She had never felt as foolish in her life as she did at that moment.

Clip-clop.

Clip-clop.

Clip-clop.

"Halloween has already passed, right?" Gwen asked.

"Gwen?" Mary called out. Her smile had faded and she looked genuinely concerned, which only amused Gwen more.

Her belly was starting to hurt, and tears were streaming down her face.

"I'm supposed to meet the perfect guy for me. My dream guy! And I look like *this*."

"We'll fix everything. Remember this is why we have trial runs," Mary said as she stepped in front of Gwen, stopping her aimless turn about the room.

Gwen's laughter also died, and she pressed her hands to her face to relieve the ache in her cheeks.

"Why don't you take a seat?" Mary said as she guided Gwen to one of the chairs in the staff room. "We have enough time to fix all of the glitches before Thursday."

Mary's megawatt smile returned, and she went on and on about the specific changes that would be made, but Gwen struggled to catch most of it. Her matchmaker sounded far away, like she was speaking to her through thick glass.

What the hell was she doing?

A dull pain pressed against Gwen's chest. She'd been trying so hard to hold off this feeling, to reason with it, to conceal it. But she'd just hit her limit.

"I don't think I can do this," Gwen said suddenly, cutting Mary off.

"The ice skating or the stroll down the Art District?"

"No, I mean don't want to do *this*," Gwen said, flailing her arms around.

"Gwen, I assure you that any dissatisfaction you're feeling is temporary. The best in the business are planning this incredible date for you—"

"I don't want to meet Mr. 96%," Gwen said.

"Why?" Mary quickly opened her tablet and started scrolling. "Is there someone else? Kento? Nelson? You rated Tyler pretty high."

As Mary continued to list different men's names, Gwen felt a pulse build in her neck. She had gone on more dates in the past two months than she had at any period in her life. But all these men, and she could barely pinpoint a standout connection or a memorable moment with any of them.

Except for one.

"Tony," Gwen said.

Mary stopped speaking and looked up. "Tony?" She scanned the list on her screen. "I don't remember anyone with that name."

Gwen's opinion of Tony had changed the day they had their accidental dinner, and she knew she officially liked him that night on her kitchen floor after she'd broken the wine glass. But she didn't know exactly when it had tipped over into something else. Something more.

But when Gwen thought of the past weeks, it was the moments she'd shared with Tony that came to mind, that made her smile. She missed him in her home. His overly serious expression obscured the sweet man beneath with a quick wit and an unassuming smile that would appear when he found something funny.

Suddenly everything grew incredibly hot, and she picked up a wayward magazine on the table in front of her to fan herself.

"I don't see a Tony," Mary said, her eyes still trained on the iPad in her hand. "Around what week did you go out with him?"

"He's not in the system," Gwen said. "He's from my real life."

"Oh, wow. Okay," Mary said, pausing for a moment before saying, "That doesn't mean you couldn't go out with this upcoming match."

Gwen shook her head. "I can't."

"Maybe we can pare down the date. Just a simple dinner and a romantic stroll will do," Mary said quickly. "We can also scrap the whole evening dress and go with something in your cl—"

"I'm in love with him."

The silence that followed stretched out for a while before Mary simply responded, "Oh."

And as Gwen sat there, she expected the words she'd

just said to curdle. To ring false. Instead, all she felt was lightness and a flutter in her chest that spurred her to act. Now.

"I have to go," Gwen said, standing up suddenly.

"Wait, right now? Can we talk—"

"No, I'm sorry," Gwen said as she kicked off the big shoes and shoved her feet back into her boots.

She quickly left the backroom, grabbing her coat and purse on the way. The front area of the beauty boutique was now bustling with clientele, but Gwen pushed her way past them to the door.

"Gwen, wait!" Mary called out from behind.

Gwen stopped, sure her matchmaker would try to convince her to stay and think about Mr. 96%, but instead, the woman held out a packet of makeup wipes and said, "For your face. Good luck."

Chapter Twenty

GWEN ENTERED SPOTLIGHT, holding her cumbersome dress in both fists. Her pulse raced as she scanned the foyer teeming with eager gym-goers. When she didn't see Tony amongst them, she made her way to the staff room.

But he wasn't there either.

On her way back to the front to ask one of the trainers at the reception desk about Tony's whereabouts, she came face-to-face with her brother, who'd just stepped out of a room into the hallway where she stood.

"Hey, what're you doing here?" Duncan asked, giving her dress a confused look. "Why you dressed like that?"

"Do you know where Tony is?"

"Hi to you too," Duncan said.

"I need to speak with Tony," Gwen said with a frantic edge in her voice.

"He's not in today. He's downtown filming for *I Choose You!*"

Gwen's heart stalled for a moment. "I-I thought he wasn't doing that."

"He changed his mind," her brother said before frowning. "Hey, you seem off. You okay?"

She nodded as she forced herself to take deep breaths. The impulsive energy that had propelled her to come to the gym in the first place was waning, leaving her feeling a bit sick.

"You wanna leave a message or something?" Duncan asked.

"No, if I'm going to do it, I should do it in person."

She'd been so caught up in the revelation of her own feelings that she hadn't even considered that Tony might not feel the same way. Sure, they got along and had great sex, but that might be where it ended for him. And here she was about to confess her lov—

"Holy fuck," her brother suddenly said. "You and Anthony."

"What—"

"I can't believe I didn't see it before," her brother said, laughing. "You're *her*. You're the mystery woman."

Gwen shook her head, confused. "Who?"

"You have feelings for Anthony."

It wasn't a question.

"How do you—"

"What're you still doing here?" her brother asked.

"What?"

"You have to go tell him."

"But you just told me he's filming *I Choose You!*," she said as Duncan took hold of her arm and proceeded to walk her down the hallway and through the foyer. "Duncan, what the hell are you doing?" Gwen asked, smacking her brother across the shoulder. "Let go of me."

But he didn't until they were both standing outside of the gym.

"You have to crash the filming set," Duncan said

without a hint of jest.

Gwen blinked.

"Right now. Get in your car and head downtown and go tell Anthony how you feel."

"But—"

"There's no 'but,'" her brother said.

"I-I can do it tomorrow."

"Tomorrow? You mean the tomorrow when he could be struck by lightning?"

"Jesus. That's fucking dark."

"Or he could meet someone today on that show he's on," Duncan continued.

Everything inside Gwen rattled at her brother's words. The idea of Tony being with someone else, choosing someone else, made her nauseous.

Without another word to Duncan, she got in her car and set her sights on downtown. But the closer she got, the relentless construction and detours frustrated Gwen until she pulled up and parked on a random curbside.

She hopped out of her car and looked around for street signs and the different high-rise buildings to orient herself.

When that failed, she turned to a woman smoking a cigarette outside a sushi restaurant in front of her and asked, "Where's the *Cup of Joe Morning Show* studio?"

The woman pointed to her left and said, "Nice dress."

"Thank you," Gwen replied before taking off at a brisk walk down the sidewalk.

The wet asphalt splashed water against her dress as she walked, and the icy air hit her skin like razor blades, but she didn't stop even to button up her coat. In fact, with all the anticipation and hope rushing through her veins, her pace soon increased until she was full-on running.

She hiked up her skirt and moved her legs faster, hopping over a puddle and dodging a man with his dog.

She didn't care that she would most likely have to pay for the dress's dry cleaning; she just kept running. In less than five minutes, she arrived in front of the studio out of breath and with ice-cold fingers and toes.

Gwen found an empty roped-off line leading to a door, and without taking time to let her heart rate settle, she strode right up to it and knocked.

At first, it was polite, but she realized that anyone on the other side of the heavy door would struggle to hear her. So she lifted both her fists and started banging as hard as she could manage.

A fleeting thought about how ridiculous she looked crossed her mind, but she kept on pounding the door until it opened to reveal a woman with pink hair wearing a headset.

Without even making eye contact with Gwen, the woman on the other side of the door said, "We're not admitting any more audience members for today's taping."

"No, I'm not here—"

The door shut with a resounding clang, and Gwen stared at the dark surface for a while, feeling a little stunned.

Before she could even think of a different option, she raised her fists and began knocking once again. When the door opened this time, the pink-haired woman reappeared but this time with her eyebrows stitched together.

"Please, hear me out," Gwen said. "I know you're filming *I Choose You!* today—"

"If you want to be considered for casting, go to our website to apply," the woman said before shutting the door for the second time.

"No," Gwen shouted and immediately started knocking. She would at least get to finish her damn sentence.

The pink-haired lady nearly pulled the door off its

hinges when she confronted Gwen once more. "Ma'am, you've got to go."

"Can you please hear me out first?" Gwen said.

Pink-haired lady huffed and planted her hands on her hips. "What is it?"

"I need to talk to Anthony Woods."

"You want to speak to the bachelor?"

"Yes."

The pink-haired woman laughed. "Impossible. He's going on stage in fifteen minutes or so."

"All I need is five."

"I'm sorry, I can't. I won't. And if you bang on this door again, I'll open it next time with security."

The door slammed on Gwen's face, and she took a moment to lean against the side of the building and catch her breath and collect herself.

She felt deflated, not to mention cold. And she was trying very hard not to think of the women inside waiting to vie for Tony's heart.

She'd been so caught up with her silly List and what she thought she wanted in a man that she'd missed what was right in front of her. How had she been so obtuse?

The door Gwen stood next to was suddenly thrown open, and she ducked her head thinking it might be the pink-haired lady returning to check if she had left. Her lungs were still screaming, but Gwen held her breath and prepared herself to run. The last thing she needed was her students' parents reading the headline, *Schoolteacher arrested for trespassing on private property of local morning talk show.*

And just as she pushed herself off the wall, a voice, a familiar one, one that had been floating in her head for weeks, said, "Gwen?"

———

"If you could have any superpower, what would you choose and why?" Anthony asked his reflection.

He stood in the green room waiting to get called onto the set of *I Choose You!* where he'd assume the titular role.

He'd been in the studio since the early morning, trapped in the small room for the majority of that time. No one warned him that filming a thirty-minute segment would require so much waiting.

In that time, he'd been able to conjure up every possible mistake he could make on stage. And despite all his efforts to muster some enthusiasm, he felt unimaginably exhausted.

He looked down at the cue cards he'd been provided. Fatigue had rendered most of the words meaningless, but he continued to reread them anyway.

He leaned closer to the mirror and peered at his reflection, and asked himself again, "If you could have any superpower, what would you choose and why?"

The response was his perfected image courtesy of the hair and makeup department.

"How're you holding up?" Janice, a producer for the segment, asked as she appeared suddenly in the room.

"Pretty good," Anthony said, backing away from the mirror like he hadn't just been talking to himself.

"Great, we'll get on set very soon. Fifteen minutes or so," Janice said.

But Anthony knew by now that that wasn't a real estimation. Everything took "fifteen minutes or so."

A voice emanated from the walkie-talkie Janice gripped in her hand, requesting her presence on set.

"On my way," Janice replied before giving Anthony a salute and zipping out of the room, her pink hair flying back behind her.

Anthony was again left alone with his thoughts, so he

grabbed a donut from the box he'd slowly been chipping away at all morning and dropped into the chair in front of the brightly lit mirror.

Months ago, if someone had said he would soon find himself in a stuffy suit getting ready to participate in a dating show, he might've laughed himself into a hernia.

But here he was in the same studio as three women who were, according to Janice, "super-duper excited to meet him."

He was glad he had the gym's publicity efforts to keep him invested in the day, otherwise who knows if he would even be in the building.

His head was still consumed with thoughts of Gwen to a degree he was embarrassed to admit. Just this morning, as he made his way in the cold from the parkade to the studio, he'd spotted a woman he could've sworn was Gwen, stepping onto the bus.

He wandered closer, tracking the woman's movements through the large vehicle, and it wasn't until she sat down and he saw her face that he realized she wasn't Gwen at all.

"You getting on, mister?" the bus driver had asked him.

Anthony had stepped back from where he'd been hovering near the door and shook his head. It was safe to say this little experience wouldn't help him get over Gwen.

"Shit," Anthony said as he returned to the present moment and looked down at the pink donut icing he'd accidentally smeared on the front of his shirt.

He left the green room for the washroom, where he used damp paper towels to roughly rub the stain.

Amid this chore, someone from the urinal section came over to the sinks to wash his hands. Anthony did a double-take when he realized the man standing next to him was Russell.

"The toilet in my dressing room isn't working," Russell explained in his "Australian" accent as he washed his hands.

Anthony nodded but resumed rubbing his shirt he was decidedly making worse with each pass.

"I have something for that," Russell said to Anthony before shouting, "Tom!"

A man wearing a turtleneck and carrying a crossbody bag entered the bathroom, looking as startled as Anthony.

"Give him the stain remover stick," Russell blithely instructed.

Anthony watched as the man with the bag quickly retrieved the stick and passed it to him.

"Thanks," Anthony said and went in on the stain and watched it slowly disappear.

"God, I hate filming these segments," Russell said as he inspected his cuticles.

"I'm sure the money's great, though," Anthony replied dryly before he could stop himself.

Russell laughed. "You're right, mate. The money is great." With a final tug at his cuffs, the talk show host pulled out a cigarette box and said, "Gotta get a quick durry in before they call me onto set."

And Anthony, with a newly stain-free shirt, returned the remover stick to the assistant.

"Oh, and if you want my advice, go with contestant number one. Real smoke show," Russell said before leaving.

Anthony frowned at the man's retreating back.

This could not be how he was spending his morning.

Once he'd made sure nothing else was out of place, Anthony left the restroom and was heading back to the green room when a very flushed production assistant approached him.

"There you are," the PA said, breathless. "We've got to get you miked up and on stage."

"Wait, we're going now?" Anthony asked.

"Yes, right now."

Everything from then on happened fast.

A makeup artist appeared from nowhere with a brush to tap on his face. Someone pulled on his suit jacket, and another deftly affixed his mic. It wasn't long before the PA was guiding him to set.

"You'll be on the left side of the stage, and the women will be on the right," the PA said as they neared their destination.

Anthony could hear the audience now. Their energy and excitement were palpable and unnerving. Things suddenly seemed real. He'd be on stage interviewing women in hopes of going on a date with one of them in a matter of minutes.

But before he could make it to the expertly lit stage, Anthony stopped dead in his tracks and said, "I need to take a moment."

"What?" the PA said, somehow getting redder. "We have to get you—"

"I'll be quick. I just need some air," he said, already turning. His tie felt too tight, and he could barely get in a full breath, but the neon exit sign in the distance was the buoy that he practically ran toward.

When he burst out of the building into a back alley, the cool air hit his hot skin, and he felt like he could finally think clearly.

All he had to do was smile, articulate his words, and breathe.

He would wring out the last of his fifteen minutes of fame, and then he could fade back into obscurity.

Anthony rolled his shoulders, took a big inhale and

exhale, and turned to reenter the studio. But movement off to his side caught his attention.

A woman wearing a light, frilly dress covered in speckles of mud stood against the wall. His heart started pounding as he took in her short haircut, dark skin, and angular profile.

He shook his head, feeling like he was once again hallucinating Gwen's presence.

There'd be no reason for her to be here, but yet he couldn't help but call out, "Gwen?"

When the woman looked over at him, he was confronted with big brown eyes that mirrored his surprise.

"W-what are you doing here?" he asked, taking in Gwen's beautiful countenance. He was positive his voice was too loud for how close they were, but he could barely hear anything with how fast the blood rushing in his ears was.

"I'm here for you," she said, her words coming out in a breathless flow.

"You came to watch the show?" he asked, knowing that would make things worse for him but wanting nothing more. It had to be better than what her absence had done to him.

"No, actually, I don't want you to go up on that stage."

He shook his head, not understanding. "Why?"

She shut her eyes and rubbed the bridge of her nose, her worry apparent in the slant of her brows.

"Gwen, what's wrong?" he asked, taking a step forward but balling his hands into fists so as not to touch her.

She looked up and met his gaze before taking an obvious breath and saying, "I'm in love with you."

Several seconds passed as the words she said worked their way to his brain to be sorted and comprehended. And it only took a few moments more for his heart to feel suddenly too big for his chest, like it might find its way outside his body.

Gwen was in love with him.

Spurred by her revelation, Anthony closed the distance between them, cupped Gwen's face in both hands, and gently pressed his lips to hers for a kiss that felt like fireworks in a dark sky, glorious and exhilarating.

Her eyes were still closed when he pulled back, and he waited until she was looking at him before saying, "I've been in love with you for a long time."

Gwen's mouth fell open, and in a voice that was barely above a whisper, said, "Bullshit."

He stroked the curve of her jaw with his thumb. "It was as close to love at first sight as it gets."

A smile grew on Gwen's face until that beautiful dimple appeared. She grabbed him by the lapels of his jacket and pulled him in for a kiss, and as their lips melded, the noise around them faded into an indistinguishable hum.

He tried to communicate everything he'd felt for her over the years, but he suspected it would take him a while to do those feelings justice.

Somewhere in the background, a squeaky voice poked through their bubble. He tried to ignore it, but Gwen broke their kiss, and they both turned to look at Janice, who stood, mouth agape, looking between them.

"You're needed on stage right now," the producer said. "We have to start filming."

For the first time in what felt like weeks, Anthony laughed.

Consequences be damned.

"Yeah, that's not happening," he said, and he got straight back to kissing the most incredible woman in the world.

Epilogue

Several Months Later

"GOD, IT'S SO BIG," Gwen said.

"I don't think it'll fit," Tony said.

Gwen tilted her head as if that would give her a new perspective. "It might. But you'd have to go in slow and maybe at an angle?"

The sales associate who'd been standing silently next to them as they debated the dimensions of the couch in front of them stepped forward and said, "If you download the store's app, you can virtually see how all the furniture looks in your home."

Gwen gave the sofa another look before turning to Tony and asking, "What do you think, babe?"

Tony's heavy shoulders rose in a sigh. "You want me to be honest?"

"Well, yeah. It's a couch for your apartment," she said.

They'd been dating for four months now, and she was happy. Like, "she loses herself while watching him cook or while they're doing their respective work in one of their living rooms" happy.

So it wasn't the end of the world that the only thing she hated about Tony was his sofa. It was made of hard, unbreathable material, and it felt like it was doing them a favor by staying intact. But they were playing Russian roulette. One day, Gwen was sure of it, the couch would collapse underneath them.

"It looks weird," Tony finally said of the couch with the contemporary shape.

"What about this one?" the sales attendant asked, moving them along to the next sofa.

It looked soft and plush, something you'd lose hours to if you weren't careful.

"Is this the only color?" Tony asked, studying the dark fabric in front of him with mild distaste.

"No, it also comes in olive green, mustard yellow, and oatmeal."

"Perfect, three different shades of vomit," Tony whispered for Gwen's ear only.

"Okay, a touch less honesty," Gwen said, squeezing his bicep.

They'd traveled out of their way to get to this department store and had spent time wading through the expansive collection of beds, shiny refrigerators, and living room furniture. They should at least leave with something.

"Could we have a moment?" Tony asked the sales attendant, who immediately nodded and disappeared.

Gwen watched as her boyfriend slumped onto the couch and ran his hand over the fabric. She could already picture herself tucked in beside him.

"I like this one," Gwen declared when she realized Tony was just being a hardass, and she might as well impose her opinion.

"What happened to it being *my* couch?" he asked.

"Well," she said, walking closer to him until she was standing between his open legs, "seeing as you'll probably fuck me on it, I feel I should have a say."

A smile tugged at the corner of his wide lips. "Is that a rule or something?"

"Yes. 'Thou shall let thy girlfriend choose the style of couch she'll get fucked on.' It comes right after the part about stealing and lying."

Without warning, Tony grabbed her arm and pulled her into his lap.

His strong arms locked around her waist as he stared into her eyes. She couldn't even feel embarrassed about the public display of affection or how obnoxious they undoubtedly looked.

"So your case for this couch is?" he asked.

"It's comfortable, affordable, and spacious."

"And you can imagine us—"

"Eating pie while we watch wholesome network sitcoms, yes," she said, nodding innocently.

He laughed, a rich, melodic sound.

"What?" she asked as his hold on her tightened slightly, and he looked at her with an odd expression.

"Nothing," he said. "Just thinking about how I completely lucked out with you."

Something warm and full bloomed where her heart was. "Well, I can't say I'm not reaping the benefits."

Only time would tell what was in store for them as a couple, but as she wrapped her arms around his neck and pressed her lips to his, she couldn't ignore the lightness in her chest that told her everything would be all right. Perfect, even.

A NOTE TO READERS

Thank you so much for reading *What a Match*! I had a lot of fun writing a hero who pines for the heroine from the start. Also, I'm glad I got to set a book during the best time of year, fall!

I sincerely hope you enjoyed Gwen and Anthony's story! If you did, let your romance-loving friends and family know about it. Again, thank you!

Mimi <3

ALSO BY MIMI GRACE

Lovestruck Series:

Book 1: *Make a Scene*

Book 2: *What a Match*

Book 3: coming soon

Standalone:

Along for the Ride

ABOUT THE AUTHOR

Mimi Grace credits the romance genre for turning her into a bookworm as a teen. She now writes sexy romantic comedies in hopes they keep others reading until late at night. Besides books, she loves generous servings of mint chocolate chip ice cream, long-running reality competition TV shows, and when she spells "necessary" correctly.

www.mimigracebooks.com

Printed in Great Britain
by Amazon